WAR GIRL URSULA

WAR GIRLS, BOOK 1

MARION KUMMEROW

CONTENTS

READER GROUP

Marion's Reader Group

Sign up for my reader group to receive exclusive background information and be the first one to know when a new book is released.

http://kummerow.info/subscribe

CHAPTER 1

Berlin, January 1943

Ursula Klausen looked through misty eyes at the steel helmet beside her. A tear slid down her cheeks as she listened to the marriage registrar ask, "Do you Ursula Klausen take Andreas Hermann to be your lawfully wedded husband?"

"Yes," she answered, struggling to keep her voice steady. She tucked an imaginary strand of her shoulder-length blonde hair behind her ear and reached her hand out, sliding her fingertips over the hard and cold steel.

She wouldn't receive an answer from the helmet, and her fiancé was far away on the Eastern Front, unable to obtain leave for his own wedding. It made her so sad. She imagined her beloved Andreas sitting next to a veil instead of his bride at that very moment. Her chest constricted. When two people in love married, they should be together.

The marriage registrar at the *Standesamt* continued with the formalities, reading the groom's agreement to marry her before asking the two witnesses to sign the marriage certificate.

Ursula put the golden wedding band on her finger and lapsed into her thoughts. This should have been the happiest day in her life, but the war had ruined everything. It had yanked Andreas from her side and thrust him into the trenches, leaving her to worry about him every second.

She sighed and glanced around the small office at the guests present. Her soon-to-be mother-in-law, an elderly cousin, her mother, solemn as a nun, and her two sisters, Anna and Lotte, who both smiled as brightly as they could muster. The smiles vanished when they looked in unison at Ursula, and as one, they looked away.

A prick of anger stabbed through Ursula. It wasn't that she had lost faith in the Führer or the war effort. Quite the contrary. The Führer had assured the German populace that the defeat at Stalingrad was only a temporary setback, and Ursula believed him. No, she clung to his words with every fiber of her being. It was as if believing Hitler's words would ensure Andreas' safe return home. To her, his wife.

But at the same time, doubts crept into her heart. The war had stolen away the men in her life. Her father, a man in his forties – whose white-blonde hair and electric blue eyes she'd inherited – wasn't there to hand her over or brush his scratchy lips against her cheek. He had always been Ursula's pillar of strength and protection. It tore her heart into pieces to know that he now fought out there in the blizzards of the harsh Soviet winter along with her younger brother, Richard.

Richard. He was hardly more than a boy with his seventeen years. They'd torn him and his friends from school, thrusting them into war. Nothing more than a bunch of schoolboys who were unprepared for the hardships and cruelties at the front.

A small smile tugged at her lips as she remembered Richard the day before he left. His uniform two sizes too big for his lanky body. The blonde hair tousled as he donned the helmet and tried a crooked smile to calm his mother's nerves.

Mutter hadn't voiced her worry or her fear, and her face had shown the same solemn expression as it did today. Nevertheless, Ursula had sensed her mother's devastation over sending her baby into the fight.

"...I declare you Mrs. Ursula Hermann." The voice of the official catapulted her back to the present. She got up and received the congratulations of the few guests.

Mutter embraced her for a few moments and then held her at arm's length. "You look lovely, my dear."

"Thanks, Mutter. Anna and Lotte have been a great help." Ursula smiled and waved at her sisters. Anna, younger by one year, had pinned Ursula's blonde waves back and given her a creamy red lipstick. The color enhanced her lips into satisfyingly perfect points at her cupid's bow and the color contrasted nicely with her electric blue eyes.

Both Anna and Lotte had chipped in with their clothing ration cards to allow Ursula to buy a new dress and handbag for her big day. She looked down at the dark blue woolen A-line skirt that ended mid-calf and the fitted jacket in the same color. The only reference to her special occasion was a white lace scarf draped casually around her shoulders. Her mother had surprised her with this precious memento she'd seamed from an old curtain.

Ursula had always been proud of her small waist and her curvy hips, but as she smoothed her hands down the skirt, there was nothing but bones beneath. While the government provided enough rations for everyone to be filled, they certainly didn't allow putting on fat.

Alles Gute," her mother-in-law wished her well with a formal handshake. The woman was understandably at a loss for words at the peculiar situation. Her son couldn't be present at his own wedding. Neither could her husband, who was missing in action.

The elderly cousin dabbed with a spotless white handkerchief at her eyes and quickly turned away. Marrying in this way drew the realities of war to the surface, a reality every woman – and man – in Berlin did their best to suppress. Ursula sighed. As much as she supported the Führer's vision to make Germany great again, she hated the side effects it involved. A wedding without the groom.

"I'm so happy for you." Her youngest sister rushed into her arms, her face surrounded by flames of untamed ginger curls. Lotte wasn't like other girls. She didn't care much about her looks, and even less about keeping a tidy and lady-like appearance. Recently turned sixteen, she still behaved like a six-year-old, a wildcat that refused to conform to social standards and believed a girl could do anything a boy could.

"Thanks, Lotte," Ursula murmured.

"But you really don't look like a bride at all," Lotte said and held her at arm's length.

"Don't say that, Lotte," Mutter chided her with a raised brow, "Ursula looks lovely. You don't need a white gown to be a bride. What counts is what's inside your heart."

Lotte pouted and opened her mouth for a retort, but closed it again at the raising of her mother's other eyebrow. That look could stop a bear in mid-charge.

"Come on, ladies, we have one hour to celebrate." Anna linked arms with Ursula. Only one year apart, the two of them had been inseparable since childhood, despite their differences in character.

The three sisters walked down the stairs arm in arm, the other three women a few steps behind.

Once Mutter was out of earshot, Lotte raised her voice again. "Why didn't you wait until Andreas came home? It was awfully strange, your wedding. Now you're married to a steel helmet," she said with a giggle.

Anna shot her a stern glance. "Ursula had her reasons. If you haven't noticed, there's a war going on."

"As if anyone could not have noticed…that stupid war is the cause of all evil. In fact, our so-called Führer is the cause of all evil. Without his oversized ego and determination to conquer every country around us, oppressing innocent people, we wouldn't have to live through all this shit," Lotte exclaimed, her voice higher-pitched with every word.

"Shush," Anna and Ursula said in unison, exchanging concerned looks.

Seconds later, the voice of their mother came from behind them. "Charlotte Alexandra Klausen, do I have to wash out your mouth with soap?"

Lotte knew as well as her sisters that talking back when Mutter used her full name would get her into hot water.

"No, Mutter, I'm sorry," she whispered, the glance she slid her sisters contradicting her words. By the time they'd reached the ground floor, Lotte couldn't hold back her curiosity. "So why the rush? Are you expecting?"

"Of course not." Ursula shot her sister an indignant look. "And what do you know about these things anyway? You're much too young for that."

"I know enough, alright. Aunt Lydia is always expecting after Uncle Peter comes home for leave." Lotte showed off her wisdom. She had lived with her aunt in the countryside for the past two years and seen her become pregnant twice.

Anna stifled a grin and turned toward her mother and the two other women. "Lotte and I have saved up our ration cards, and we're inviting everyone for cake and *Ersatzkaffee*."

Ursula squeezed Anna's arm in gratitude for the distraction. As much as she loved her youngest sister, her uninhibited speech was taxing, to say the least. Lotte blurted out what she thought and never considered the consequences, nor the feelings of others.

It wasn't that Ursula hadn't asked herself that same question many times over. The reason she went forward with the wedding was that she wanted to make sure neither of them died before they were married. It sounded morose, but it was the truth. During these awful times, death lingered around every corner, and nobody could trust to live to the next day. She wanted – no she needed – to be united with Andreas in matrimony. Now, their love couldn't be destroyed, not even by death.

Mrs. Ursula Hermann.

Her new name evoked a small smile. Andreas wasn't here with her, but his name was. It strengthened their bond and showed to everyone she was his. She would be a respectable soldier's wife. At the age of twenty-two, it was high time for her if she didn't want to end up an old spinster. Of course, their marriage also had some more practical aspects. It had been Andreas' idea, and she'd first opposed it. He'd wanted to ensure she'd be taken care of should the worst happen. In case of his demise, she'd be secured and receive a widow's pension.

A longing tugged at her heart as her mind wandered to her *secret* reason for the wedding. She wanted to be prepared for the time Andreas got leave. Mutter would never allow her unwed daughter to spend time alone with a man. But now, she couldn't deny Ursula's husband the right to share the bed with his wife.

Heat rushed to her cheeks, and she hoped nobody would be able to read her mind. A baby. That's what she wanted. It would give her an excuse to leave her dreadful job.

"What do you want?" Anna's voice cut through her romantic ideas.

"Me?" Ursula looked up, confused. With her thoughts so far away, she hadn't noticed that they'd entered the bakery, and she was standing in front of the counter staring at the sweet delicacies. Compared to pre-war times, it was a miserable display, but still, her heart jumped at the unfamiliar sight of sugary sweets.

"Hmm." She inhaled the scent of baked pastries, her eyes raking from one piece to the next. Andreas loved *Sahnetorte*, cake made of different layers of custard and cream. Ursula licked her lips and remembered a scene before he was drafted off to war. He had covered his finger with whipped cream and spread it on her nose. Then he'd kissed it off.

But there was no *Sahnetorte* in the display.

"I'll take a *Pfannkuchen*," she said and sat at one of the tables while Anna organized everything. Minutes later, Anna and the baker's wife brought six cups of steaming *Ersatzkaffee* and six plates with sweets.

Ursula bit into her deep-fried bun, covered with a whiff of powdered sugar and filled with delicious strawberry jam.

After several minutes filled with careless chatter, Ursula glanced at the clock on the wall. "I'm sorry I have to leave for work." Both she and Anna had received half a day's leave for her wedding.

"Me too. Let's walk together to the tram," Anna said and kissed her mother on the cheek before she bid her goodbyes to Andreas' mother and the neighbor.

"See you tonight, Mutter." Ursula leaned over, and much to her surprise, her mother squeezed her hands tight.

"I'm sorry, my darling. Once the war is over, you'll get a proper wedding. Church, groom, gown, and everything," Mutter said with a slight tremble in her voice. It was one of the rare occasions her mother showed emotion, and it filled Ursula's heart with – with what? Comfort? Despair?

"Are you happy?" Anna asked as they linked arms and left the bakery to catch the tram.

"I am. Somewhat. But who can be truly happy with this war going on?"

Anna nodded and sighed. "It will all get better. One day. We have us. And our work to keep us from overthinking."

"At least you like your job. But my soul-destroying work as a prison guard? I wish I could resign."

"You can resign and ask the authorities to put you to another task," Anna reminded her.

"If the Führer believes this work is where I serve my country best, then who am I to argue?"

Anna rolled her eyes. They'd had this discussion countless times. Anna had fought tooth and nail to go to university and study human biology. Becoming a scientist was unheard of for a girl. *Inappropriate*, Mutter had said. *You will never find a husband*, she'd added. And Vater had nodded.

Ursula giggled at the memory. In the end, Anna had relented and opted for training as a registered nurse. Mutter and Vater had sighed with relief upon their daughter's change of mind. Only Ursula knew that the nurse training was part of her sister's larger plan to become financially independent and enroll in university without her parent's consent after the war.

In contrast to Anna, Ursula never fought. She prided herself in accepting her fate with grace. She did what was expected of her. Like any good daughter and woman, she obeyed her parents and her government. Soon, she would obey her husband. That was just the way life was.

The authorities had determined that her part of the home effort was to be a prison guard. Whether she liked it or not wasn't important. Sacrifices must be made for the greater good. And as much as her stomach clenched every time she entered that dreadful place, she would bear it with fortitude.

Until she was expecting. Then she would have a valid reason to resign. Then she would become a proud and happy mother.

"See you tonight." Ursula kissed her sister on the cheek as each one caught a tram going in opposite directions.

She leaned her head against the window and glanced

outside. They passed rubble and destruction on the way to her prison. The awfulness of war couldn't be escaped. The Nazi regime had done so much good for Germany and the Germans over the years, the war was a minor sacrifice on the way to greatness.

In her childhood, before the new Führer, the streets of Berlin were a constant gray, people blurring into the buildings. Money became little more than a rumor, and faces showed nothing but sorrow. As time went on, the Führer lifted Germany out of its despair. The streets sprung to life, as though a sudden explosion of color had painted the world in roses. Of course, this prosperity was now tainted with conflict. But Goebbels never forgot to mention in his speeches that this was only temporary. Great things awaited those who were worthy.

Ursula wanted to be worthy.

CHAPTER 2

"I'm home!" Ursula called over her shoulder as she arrived at the apartment after her shift. The radio blared in her mother's empty room.

"...an English bomb squadron entering German airspace. The predicted route is Gardelegen..."

Ursula sighed as she closed the door and glanced at the two suitcases in the hallway. One of them contained documents, ration cards, and clothing for the three women, while the other one was stuffed with bottles of water and non-perishable food. They might have to use them tonight – again. When the radio mentioned the city of Gardelegen, the bombers were almost always destined to Berlin.

The voices of Mutter and her sisters drew her to the kitchen.

"It's awful," she heard Anna's distinct low voice say, "and ironic, don't you think?"

Lotte cut in impatiently, "It's not awful, it's stupid! What are they gaining? Dead is dead, it's just sadistic to be determined to do it yourself. *I* think–"

Ursula swung open the door and interrupted the conversation, "What has happened? What's awful?"

Anna slid Lotte a look that said *Shut up, this is my territory.* Ursula couldn't help but smile. Her two sisters were both strongly opinionated, willing to go against anyone and anything in their way. They'd butted heads more often than she cared to remember, and as the oldest one, it had always been her task to mediate between them.

Some things never changed. Not even living in the countryside with their Aunt Lydia for the past two years, far away from Berlin and the dangers of war, had managed to soften Lotte's hot-blooded outbursts.

"We are talking about one of my patients in the Moabit prison hospital," Anna explained. "He was convicted of treason, a spy or something, and has been sentenced to death."

A shudder ran down Ursula's spine at her sister's words. Despite having seen every kind of criminal at the prison, she still couldn't stomach the idea of sentencing those persons to death. They were humans, after all.

"But he tried to commit suicide. Instead of being happy that he saved them the dreadful task, the prison guards sent him straight to hospital. All of us are doing everything we can to save his life, and either no one has thought about it, or everyone is too scared to mention the fact that, well, he's going to die anyway." Anna gave a dark laugh, a sick kind of humor.

"So, what will happen to him?" Ursula asked, "Will he be all right?"

Lotte interjected, "He'll be all right until they kill him. Honestly, what a ridiculous system. Our entire government is a sick joke!"

The room went so silent one could hear a pin drop. One glance at Mutter's face told Ursula it was high time for an intervention.

Turning a pointed look upon Lotte, Ursula said, "So, tell us about Aunt Lydia and the countryside." Aunt Lydia was Mutter's youngest sister. At seventeen, she'd married the son of a farmer and moved with him to a god-forsaken village that even used the word village in its name. Kleindorf. Tiny village. At thirty years of age, she had turned into a robust farmer's wife, her long, thick blonde hair braided into snails above her ears. She'd born eight children, five of whom had survived, and her answer to every problem was discipline.

"Aunt Lydia is very strict," Lotte complained with a pouty lower lip. "She won't let me do anything fun."

"It can't be that bad. How are our cousins?" Anna asked.

"They are nice. I like Maria the best. She'll turn one next month. And although Aunt Lydia hasn't said anything, everyone can see she's getting fat again."

"Charlotte Alexandra," Mutter chided her and got up to offer Ursula a cup of tea. "Are you hungry, darling? There's some left-over casserole in the oven."

"Thanks, Mutter." Ursula grabbed a plate and sat at the table to eat her food.

"When are you going back to Kleindorf?" Anna asked.

Mutter flashed her eyes, indicating this was a sensitive subject.

"I'm not going back," Lotte stated with finality in her voice and rose from the table.

"Lotte, we have discussed this. It's for your own safety. The Führer has asked anyone not necessary for the war effort to leave Berlin. With those..." Mutter shot a look upwards, "annoying English aircraft, you're better off with your aunt in the countryside."

Come on, Mutter. Call them bloody damn murderers, like everyone else does.

"I said..." Lotte took a deep breath as if calming herself, "that I am *not* leaving. This is my home. You are my family. I hate the countryside. It's boring there, and no one has half a brain. I need actual conversation, from someone other than a snotty child or a cud-chewing cow."

"Well, maybe I should come with you then. I haven't seen Lydia and my nephews and nieces in ages. Anna and Ursula can cope on their own for a while, and I can provide some *actual* conversation for you," Mutter said with a hint of a smile as she saw the look of half-masked horror on her daughter's face.

Anna spoke up, "That's a great idea. You'll both be much safer out of Berlin. And you can send us some of Aunt Lydia's delicious cheese and ham."

Lotte paced the kitchen poking her tongue out at her sister behind her mother's back. "It's a bad idea. And I do not need to be taken care of. I'm not a child anymore."

Ever pragmatic, Anna did not rise to Lotte's bait. "I'm referring to that very attitude. Not to mention your inability to keep your opinions to yourself. Do you not understand what could happen if people heard the comments you make about the Nazis and our Führer?"

"So, am I supposed to ignore what the Nazis are doing to our country? To our people? Our country has become a place of horror. We should be fighting against the Nazis, not shutting up and looking away. Aren't you sick and tired of seeing all those cruelties? Don't you want it to end? Where's your conscience?" Lotte all but shouted into the kitchen, picking up speed in her pacing.

Her sisters and Mutter looked at one another. Ursula's stomach clenched. She'd seen time and again what happened to criminals. And people who didn't agree with the National Socialists were considered criminals.

Mutter's face paled with angst as she pressed her lips into a thin line.

"What? Are you too frightened to hear the truth?" Lotte challenged them, pursing her lower lip.

"Charlotte Alexandra Klausen. Do not let me hear you say that ever again. This behavior got you expelled from the *Bund Deutscher Mädel* two years ago, and it was only your tender age and Vater's intervention that saved you from God knows what..." Mutter's stare could have cut through steel as she chided her youngest daughter. "It doesn't matter whether I agree with your political opinions or not. What matters to me is your safety. You're sixteen now, and your father is not here to save you. If the wrong person overhears what you're saying, you will end up in prison. Ask Ursula if you don't believe me."

"Mutter," Ursula murmured, squirming in her chair.

"Tell your sister what happens to those who are considered political opponents," Mutter drove home her point with a voice that allowed no protest.

"Arrest. Torture. Prison. Possibly a death sentence," Ursula murmured as she glanced down at her clasped hands. When she dared to look at her sister's face, Lotte's demeanor had changed. She still pouted, but her shoulders hunched forward and fear darkened her beautiful green eyes.

Mutter rose and closed the distance to her youngest daughter. Ursula could see the determination on her face and wondered what would happen next.

"It is decided. I am coming with you to the countryside. Or you are going to get yourself into serious trouble. We will leave tomorrow."

The tension in the kitchen settled like mist, and Ursula had difficulty breathing. Lotte would not go against her mother's explicit wishes, or would she? After two years of living hundreds of kilometers away from Berlin with Aunt Lydia, she had grown from a child to a *Backfisch*, an adolescent, and a fiery one.

But Lotte had no opportunity to answer because a harrowing, bone-chilling sound reached their ears, and it took Ursula a second or two to realize it wasn't her sister screaming, but the air-raid sirens emitting their dreaded warning. The tension in the room snapped like a rubber band as the shrill noise filled the air, initiating an often-practiced routine.

Ursula, Anna, and Mutter jumped to their feet, and ran for the front door, grabbing the suitcases on their way out, leaving a dumbfounded Lotte frozen in place in the middle of the kitchen.

"Come on, Lotte!" Ursula shouted, but her sister stood motionless with eyes wide as saucers. Ursula returned to grab her arm and dragged her out of the apartment and down the stairs into the open. The street bustled with people like so many speeded-up Charlie Chaplins, hurrying along to reach the safety of the nearby *Hochbunker*.

The wailing sirens blotted out all other sounds but stopped the moment Ursula and Lotte darted out of the building. *Shit! Sixty seconds. We are too slow.*

"Run!" Ursula yelled with full lungs. The routine had been drilled into them so many times she could find her way with closed eyes, but it was Lotte's first alarm, and she behaved like a headless chicken. Ursula grabbed her sister tighter and started.

The spine-chilling drone of the approaching bombers crept into her bones, and she risked a glance up to the sky. A glowing *Tannenbaum,* flare bombs indicating the position where most of the bombs would be dropped, hovered in the air. It was the only light in an otherwise completely blacked-out city.

A formation of aircraft approached the lit-up target, and Ursula estimated it would be less than a minute before they started dropping their lethal charge over Berlin. *Bloody English killer pilots! Rot in hell!*

Ursula increased her pace, dragging her sister behind as the ground jumped beneath them from the deafening burst of a high-explosive bomb. She pushed her scarf over her mouth and nose to keep from breathing the thick air full of dust swirling from the buildings. She knew the drill. Explosive bombs first. Then the mines. Even hundreds of yards away, a person had slim chances of survival when hit by the destructive force of their detonation waves. Last came the dreaded phosphor bombs.

Her heart hammering against her ribs, she had one goal in mind. To reach the shelter. Beside her, she could hear Lotte's panting and feel her legs giving out. With her last ounce of strength, she hauled her sister past the safety of the bunker door. *I swear to God, if I ever lay my hands on an Englishman, I'll make him pay for this.*

Surprised at the violence of her thoughts, she stopped for a moment and bent over to catch her breath before turning to Lotte. "You all right?"

A pale face nodded in response. Ursula tucked a wild curl behind Lotte's ear. Her sister's face – and probably her own – was smeared with dust. They had been the last ones to reach the *Hochbunker* before the doors were locked for the upcoming attack. The bunker was a huge concrete building, sufficient to host five hundred people.

"Let's go." Ursula led her speechless sister to their regular place, greeting familiar faces here and there. Mutter had equipped their space with three mattresses and blankets as well as a petrol light for when the electric light failed, as it usually did many times throughout an attack.

Lotte stood shell-shocked, and Ursula saw her eyes fill with tears. She wanted to wrap her arms around her little sister, but Mutter was faster.

Anna and Ursula exchanged a glance. She remembered vividly how afraid she'd been the first few times. Since then, spending a night in the bunker had become nothing more than an annoying habit.

Ursula and Anna crouched together to make room for Lotte. It would be a long night until the all clear sign was given. Ursula huddled down to sleep and touched one of Andreas' letters that she always kept in her pocket.

In a world of fear and darkness, Andreas' words made her

laugh, and her lips tingled with the memory of his kisses. She'd read his letter so many times she knew it by heart. A wave of sadness washed over her. Despite being his wife, she couldn't expect to be reunited with him in the near future. Yet another sacrifice to make in this awful war.

My beloved Ursula,

It has been such a long time since I last saw you, but for the first time, I am relieved to be apart from you as I cannot stand to see you hurt, and it is through my own words that the hurt will be caused.

I have asked ceaselessly for leave to return to you, but the answer was no. You know as well as I do that there is very little to be done. The war is too important and every man who can fight, must.

Believe me, I want to leave everything behind and be with you – and one day we will. For now, my thoughts and my love have to suffice.

I love you. I love you more than anything in this world. And I'm anxiously waiting to wrap you in my arms as my wife.

Forever yours, Andreas

With the assurance of his love soothing her mind, she dozed off into a fitful sleep.

CHAPTER 3

The next morning, Lotte and Mutter packed their suitcases and took the tram to the train station Lehrter Bahnhof train station. The journey to Aunty Lydia's tiny village in Lower Bavaria would take most of the day and possibly the night.

While air raids had become normal, this one had reawakened the urgency for Lotte and her mother to leave Berlin for the relative safety of the countryside. Not only would they avoid the heavy bombing and warfare, but also any fallout from Lotte's sharp tongue and its tendency to cause trouble.

Anna and Ursula kissed them on the cheeks and promised to write letters every week. Then each one of them left for work. Anna to the hospital and Ursula to the prison.

The watchman at the prison entrance greeted her, "Good morning, Fräulein Klausen."

"Good morning, Herr Müller, it is Frau Hermann now," she answered with a bright smile.

"Oh. I forgot, you got marriage leave yesterday morning," the old man with a peg leg from the last war said. "Did you enjoy the time with your new husband? Young love…"

Tears shot to Ursula's eyes, and she took a deep breath to

will them away. "It was a *Stahlhelmtrauung*. He's somewhere in Russia fighting the enemy."

"I'm sorry, but you need to have faith that he'll come back soon." Herr Müller looked away, uncomfortable at the prospect of the young woman in front of him breaking out in tears.

"I will." Ursula turned to enter the gray building that always gave her the chills.

"Wait. Officer Fischer instructed me to tell you to go straight to his office as soon as you arrived."

Ursula nodded and straightened her shoulders. Entering the dreadful building *and* summoned before her superior. How much worse could this day become?

"Heil Hitler," Officer Fischer greeted her. Intimidating and stern, he was the kind of man nobody had ever seen smile. His oversized mustache hung down over his mouth as though a small willow tree grew from his nostrils.

"Heil Hitler," Ursula uttered the words, casting her eyes downward.

"Frau Hermann, thank you for coming to see me. Although I was beginning to think you would never turn up." Officer Fischer's baritone voice was monotonous, making it impossible to identify whether he was joking or not.

Ursula was often put in this awkward position and usually gave a small unenthusiastic laugh so as not to seem rude either way. Today though, she got the impression he was trying to elevate the mood.

"You are being transferred."

"Where am I going?" Ursula asked, unsurprised. Untrained personnel like her were often relocated according to the manpower needs of the different prisons. Ursula suspected the real reason was to prevent fraternizing with the prisoners. But who would want to become friends with criminals? Not her. Although some of them were kind and likable persons and

Ursula had often wondered how they'd ended up in such a place.

"Plötzensee prison," Fischer said, hiding his eyes by leafing through the nearest pile of papers that stood like a city all over his desk. "It's a men's prison, but there is a small facility for women. Subversives."

"Subversives?" Ursula swallowed.

"Yes." The disgust in his voice betrayed his unreadable face. Then he sighed, "I have asked my superiors not to transfer you, but to no avail. These are bad people. The worst. Not the common criminals we have here."

Ursula nodded, but fear crawled like spiders over her skin.

"These people are worse than the Jews because they have *chosen* to betray Führer and Fatherland. I hate the Jews as much as the next person because they come from a bad breed. It may not be the individual's fault to be born from bad blood, but we have to extirpate them anyways, as we would extirpate a weed in our garden." He paused to take a breath after his enthusiastic speech. "But I have to warn you. The subversives are the truly dangerous ones. You have to stay alert at all times and not let them dull your mind." Officer Fischer's light brown eyes gleamed in his eagerness to keep Ursula safe.

"Understood, sir," Ursula answered, cold shivers of unknown evil running down her spine. "Thank you for the warning." Still, she smiled at him with her signature mask of calm and left his office with instructions to show up at her new job the next morning.

Ursula remained lost in the labyrinth of her mind for the rest of her shift, a complex battle of emotions mirroring the war outside the prison's walls. She prided herself on her ability to stay strong and stable throughout times of tension, but today, she felt inexplicable guilt for her constant compliance.

Lotte had often shamed her for what she considered cowardice, but until now Ursula had ignored it. She never asked questions like her sisters did, but simply complied with what was expected of her. Duty was more important than fighting against the natural flow of society.

With the transfer to a prison with the worst of the worst inmates looming over her, physical strain coursed through every fiber of her body. She barely breathed as she went through her routine of unlocking and locking cell doors when bringing food or herding the women down to the courtyard during leisure hour.

I was assigned this job to best serve my country. I am doing my duty as a German citizen. Sacrifices have to be made. Ursula repeated the words over and over in her mind. But she couldn't silence the small voice in the back of her head, insisting that she could have opposed, could have requested work somewhere else.

By the time Ursula returned home, she was exhausted, depressed, and lonely. Lotte's visit had brought fun and joy during the short time she'd been with them. But it wasn't only her little sister's missing presence that turned the apartment into a quiet and eerie place. The absence of Mutter, who'd always held her hand over her daughters, loomed like a shadow inside the walls.

Anna and Ursula were alone. Completely alone. At ages twenty-one and twenty-two, they'd never had to take care of themselves.

Before she could sink deeper into her morose thoughts, the door tore open with a crash, and Anna barreled inside, her hands holding two bags.

"I went by the grocery store and bought everything I could get with our ration cards, so we won't have to go shopping for the rest of the week." Anna grinned at her sister.

Ursula's face flushed with guilt as she stood from the couch and helped her sister store the provisions. As they finished,

Anna glanced at her sister's tired face and grabbed her by the wrist.

"Come on, Ursula, let's go out for a drink. Now that Mutter isn't here." She bobbed her eyebrows, looking as though she too could use some fun.

The nearest watering hole was once a thriving and modern place, but with the arrival of war, it had become shabby with neglect. The effects of the diversion of any kind of construction material to the war effort could clearly be observed in the establishment.

Ursula balked at the entrance. "What will people think if the two of us enter without an escort?" she whispered.

"They will think we desperately need a drink after spending yet another night in an air raid shelter and working our behinds off all day." Anna rolled her eyes and walked straight up to the wooden bar with her sister in tow.

Then she climbed on the slightly rickety stool in her mid-calf-length skirt, woolen stockings, and worn shoes. She neatly crossed her legs and leaned two fingers against her cheek, imitating one of Marlene Dietrich's grand poses in the film *The Blue Angel*. Ursula laughed at her sister and struggled to climb onto the stool.

"Two schnapps, please," Anna ordered from the barmaid before turning to Ursula.

"Schnapps?" Ursula raised an eyebrow but was too tired to protest. Apparently, her sister had decided to go wild now that they had escaped the stern hand of their mother.

"Sure. Had a rough day?" the barmaid asked as if it was the most normal thing in the world that two respectable young ladies walked inside the bar and ordered the hard liquor. A few moments later, she put two shot glasses with a transparent liquid in front of them.

Ursula took the glass in her hand and sniffed. The strong smell stung her eyes.

"Down it," Anna demanded and put her glass to her lips.

Ursula followed her example and downed the entire shot in one gulp. The alcoholic bite burnt through her throat all the way to her stomach, and she gasped, causing her sister to grin. But funnily enough, it left a comfortable warmth after the sting subsided.

"I'll be transferred to Plötzensee tomorrow," she murmured.

"Plötzensee? Isn't that where they keep the subversives?" her sister asked, her eyes wide.

Ursula's heart contracted. "Yes, and my superior warned me about these people."

"Most are good people," Anna answered with an air of defiance.

"How can you say that? They betrayed the Fatherland." Ursula usually didn't discuss politics, but the alcohol had lowered her inhibitions.

"Have you ever thought that maybe our government is wrong?" Anna's voice was merely a whisper, but loud enough for Ursula to glance around to see if anyone had heard. When she didn't find anyone within earshot, she relaxed.

"How can our Führer be wrong? We don't remember how terrible things were before, but Mutter and Vater do. The Führer and the Party have worked so hard to rebuild our country from the rubble it had become after the Great War and the Depression. We have enough enemies who envy our success so much that they fight against us; we don't need resistance from within." Ursula repeated what she'd been drilled at school, although she couldn't completely silence the doubts that crept into her mind more persistently with each passing day.

Even though the Nazis had perpetrated the war for good reasons, it was still a war. And it had brought death and despair to everyone in the country. How could this be a good thing? How could harassing the Jews and other Undesirables be a good thing? How could being cruel and fearsome be a good thing?

Her Catholic parents had raised Ursula with the morals and kindness of a good Christian. And although she didn't flaunt her religion like a badge of pride, she knew it was wrong to harm others, no matter the reason.

"The patient in my hospital, he's a kind man. Educated, polite, humorous. He was sentenced to death because he opposed the Nazi ideology. And just recently, a whole bunch of resisters was hanged. Hanged! Who does that? Hanging was used in the Middle Ages when people were cruel and uneducated. Haven't we learned a thing since then?" Anna's eyes glared with indignation.

Ursula remained silent because she sensed – in a way only sisters can – that Anna needed to get this off her chest.

"You may have heard about Harro Schulze-Boysen, the *Luftwaffe* officer. He was the leader of the group. I just can't...I don't see the justice. Execution for, effectively, disagreeing with our Führer?" Anna glanced at her sister with desperation.

I'm sure these people did a lot more than disagree with Hitler.

The barmaid approached, and after a glance at her sister, Ursula ordered a second round of schnapps. Every person in this hellish place called Berlin suffered breakdowns from time to time, especially when the realities struck as insurmountable. Today was Anna's day. And Ursula's task was to listen to her sister, let her whine, shout, and argue, and then bring her safely back home to accept the unacceptable.

"Look at us! We don't even have freedom of speech anymore. Look at Lotte! We were forced to send her away to the countryside for fear that she will get herself into trouble with her sharp tongue. But she's right! She speaks nothing but the blatant truth that we are all too scared to see, or admit to seeing," Anna exploded, her words hanging in the air like ash floating down. A few of the other patrons looked over.

"I'm sorry, my sister has too many sorrows to bear," Ursula

apologized, and the heads turned away. Every single one of them had too many sorrows to bear and understood.

"Anna, please lower your voice, or you'll be hanged yourself."

Anna sighed and downed the schnapps the barmaid had served. Then she giggled hysterically.

"Yes. You're right, let's talk about something fun. It's such a rare occasion when we go out and have fun. We'll do it more often now that Mutter isn't here to watch over us." Anna did one full turn on her bar stool in slow motion. When she faced her sister again, she said, "Have you noticed, there's not a single man our age in this place?"

Ursula nodded. "It's odd, isn't it?" It was already dark outside, and because of the thick blackout curtains, they couldn't look out the window. But on the short walk over, they hadn't met a young man either, save for two SS men.

"Heavens, I have almost forgotten what normal men look like. The only ones we get to see are in uniform, and their appearance makes me itch." Anna straightened her perfectly straight hair.

"You're right. Those uniformed SS or Gestapo send shivers down my spine, too. It's like when we were children, and Mutter gave us *that* look. You immediately racked your brain to remember whether you'd done something wrong."

"But you've never done anything wrong in your entire life," Anna giggled, "it was always me."

Ursula shot her a mock scowl. "Yes, but I got scolded anyways because I was the oldest. And you had that annoying ability to make everyone believe you're innocent." Ursula remembered more than one occasion where she'd received the chastisement because Anna pulled her I'm-a-sweet-and-inno-cent-girl act.

Anna guffawed. "I still have that ability. It comes in handy at times."

Ursula shook her head. "When will you grow up and stop doing things you aren't supposed to?"

"You can talk. At least you're married." Anna did another full turn on her bar stool, observing the patrons.

"And here I thought you weren't one to long for marriage. Weren't you the one complaining that the boys wouldn't leave you alone?" Ursula squinted her eyes at her sister in an effort to concentrate despite the warmth of the alcohol coursing through her.

"Oh, don't give me that look. I'm not desperate for a husband and babies, but what girl doesn't want a little romance? How am I supposed to find someone special to go out with when the few men around are only interested in finding spies and criminals? I may as well become a nun."

Ursula snorted. "Don't even consider it, you would make a terrible nun. They would kick you out faster than you could even pray. The war won't go on forever, and when it's over, everything will be like it was before."

Anna frowned and chewed on her bottom lip, looking pensive. "What if this damn war *does* go on forever...until nobody is left to return home?"

"The Führer says we are nearing the end, and besides, we have lots to look forward to when it does. There is no use in complaining about things we cannot change."

"What exactly are you looking forward to?" Anna eyed her sister suspiciously.

Ursula felt the heat rush to her cheeks at the thought of her husband. She bit her lip and then answered matter-of-factly, "Andreas. I want so badly to have a baby and finally to stop working."

"Is that all you want from life? To be a housewife and moth-er?" Disappointment was etched on Anna's face.

"Isn't that enough? What else could I want?"

"Don't you have any hopes and dreams? Any personal ambitions beyond what you could do for other people? What about yourself?" Anna wrinkled her forehead.

"No, I don't. All I want is to be happy." Ursula gave a nod toward the blackout curtains. "See that? Right now, my only ambition is to survive this war. Anything I do will be better than being a prison guard."

"You are just so perfect. You've always been the perfect daughter, the A-student, the girl who never contradicted her teachers or caused trouble…" Anna jumped from her stool, and every single pair of eyes in the room was glued to her body as she theatrically raised her arms and exclaimed, "You never scratched your knees because you fell down from a tree, or dirtied your white Sunday dress in a puddle. You never sneaked out of Mass because it was too boring. You didn't even make out with boys behind our parents' backs…"

Ursula felt the heat rushing to her face as the spectators' eyes wandered between her and Anna. "Shush…"

"I'm sick and tired of shushing! I've had enough of everyone telling me what I can and can't do! I want to live my own life. I'm done being an inferior copy of you…" Anna stood in the middle of the bar, shoulders shaking as her voice broke off.

"Anna…" Ursula embraced her sister, "Nobody wants you to be like me. And I'm far from perfect." She tried a smile but failed miserably.

"You are. Ever since I can remember, everyone has told me to be more like you. I don't want to be you!" Anna broke out in tears.

"Let's go home." Ursula paid the barmaid and then escorted her sister outside. The crisp winter air hit them and burnt their faces, but it was a welcome change from the stifling warmth inside the bar.

Ursula linked arms with her sister and watched how her own breath turned into white clouds as if she were smoking. Not that Ursula would ever do such a thing.

She sighed. "That didn't turn out too well, our plan to have fun. Did it?"

"No. Not really. I'm sorry." Anna dried her tears.

"Don't be sorry, we all need to let off steam sometimes." *Even I do, but nobody will ever witness this.*

"I'm so frustrated. It's terribly hard when every day gets you further away from your goals. I only became a nurse because it would give me a head start at studying human biology, and look at me now. Patching up patients, just to give them back to the Gestapo so they can torture them some more. Is there any more useless and horrible work than this?" Her ambitions were a sore spot in Anna's life. She'd always wanted to study biology, but her parents had flat-out denied her this wish. She was a woman and women didn't become scientists. Period.

"You'll get through this war, and then you're going to study biology, regardless of what Mutter or Vater say. I'll support you," Ursula heard herself say. Judging by her sister's facial expression, Anna was as surprised at these words as she was.

They arrived at their building and walked up the stairs. As Ursula unlocked the door to the apartment, she heard the peephole of the neighboring door click. *Doesn't that woman have anything else to do than spy on her neighbors?*

Anna had moved her things to their mother's bedroom earlier in the day, and as they said goodnight, Ursula was happy about the unusual privacy. Too many things whizzed through her head.

Both her sisters had such strong opinions and lofty goals for the future, Ursula felt weak and unimportant in comparison. But try as she might, when she closed her eyes, all she dreamed of was a peaceful life with Andreas and their children.

CHAPTER 4

The alarm rang, and Ursula stirred. Thanks to the blackout curtains, it was pitch dark in the apartment. The silence was staggering. Not even the sound of breathing came from Anna's bed.

Then she remembered. Mutter and Lotte had left, and Anna had moved to Mutter's room. As much as Ursula had craved some privacy, it was frightening to wake up alone.

She switched on the light on her nightstand and went through her morning routine. She was expected early at the new prison. Her stomach felt queasy, but it wasn't the usual sensation of repugnance for her job. It was…fear of the unknown.

Officer Fischer's warnings had created terrifying images of strong, dangerous women who would intimidate and manipulate her. Maybe even attack her. Take her hostage in an attempt to escape. Although she'd never heard of such an incident, that didn't mean those things couldn't happen.

Half an hour later, she took the bus to Charlottenburg and got off near the main entrance to Plötzensee prison. A shiver ran down her spine as she neared the building complex that was used as the central place of execution for political prisoners.

The administrative building looked innocent enough with its signature red bricks and the gracefully arched windows – or it would if it weren't for the massive steel portal and the grilled windows.

A ten-feet high brick and mortar fence in the same red color surrounded the entire compound and was topped with barbed wire to make any attempt to escape futile. On the far end of the complex stood smaller buildings, the living quarters for the permanent staff. Ursula shuddered again. The thought of living inside the prison walls wasn't exactly pleasing; at least she could go home at night.

Ursula registered in the administrative building and was then led to her new superior, Frau Schneider – a resolute woman in her fifties, her ash-blonde hair tied into a perfect chignon.

"Frau Hermann?" At Ursula's nod, she continued, "I've been expecting you. We are very short-staffed so I won't have much time to show you around. I was told you've been in another prison before?"

"Yes, Frau Schneider. I have worked in two different prisons, it won't take long to learn the routines here."

"Good." Her new superior looked Ursula up and down, taking in her figure. Then she frowned. "You're small."

"I'm five feet four," Ursula answered automatically. It was a sore spot in her life. Even her little sister had surpassed her in height this year.

"I'm afraid we don't have a uniform in your size. Usually, our employees are taller," Frau Schneider said with an unreadable face and gestured for Ursula to follow her to the staff room.

In the staff room, she handed Ursula a gray, scratchy uniform two sizes too big that consisted of a mid-calf-length skirt and a supposedly tailored jacket that bagged on her. After a disproving glance at the abysmal state of Ursula's shoes, Frau Schneider rummaged in a nearby closet and pulled out a brand-new shiny pair of black leather boots.

Ursula's eyes went wide. Even with ration cards, shoes weren't something you could buy – anywhere.

"I have no idea why they gave us children's sizes, but maybe they'll fit you," Frau Schneider commented and urged Ursula to try them on.

Ursula did as told and discarded her ill-fitting torn shoes to put on the shiny boots. They fit like gloves, soft and comfortable, and the first tentative steps she took felt like walking on clouds.

"I love them." She smiled at her superior. "Can I really have them?"

Frau Schneider nodded with the tiniest lift of a smile on her face. "Yes. Now follow me."

Several hours later, Ursula felt as if she'd been in the prison forever. There really wasn't much difference to her old one, except this one was bigger. She soon learned that the cell blocks formed a large cross, the first wing reachable via a door from the administrative building with the staff rooms. Three of the wings were reserved for men, and one for women.

During the following days, she carried out the duties that she had so long become accustomed to. Patrol, search, and treat with suspicion. This was the very essence of her work that she struggled with so much: suspicion.

Over the next days, she was surprised to discover that the political prisoners weren't the ugly criminals her former boss had warned her about. Instead, most of them were kind and warmhearted women.

One day, she accompanied a new arrival to her cell. Margit Staufer wasn't even twenty, and her round, childlike face didn't bear any resemblance to the terrifying criminal she was supposed to be.

31

According to her file, Margit hadn't even had a trial, and yet she was put on death row along with the other condemned prisoners. It was one of those occasions when Ursula questioned the supreme wisdom of her government.

The woman already in the cell, Hilde Quedlin, had been sentenced to death three days earlier and hadn't spoken a word since. As strange as it sounded, Ursula worried about her. *Maybe the company of Margit will cheer her up.*

Days turned into weeks, and Ursula's stomach stopped being queasy on her way to work. More than once, a smile appeared on her lips as she greeted the now familiar faces of *her* inmates.

In her old prison, distributing food was the most dreaded task because the guards had to enter the cells. They were always fearful of an ambush, a prisoner attacking, spitting, or calling them names.

But when Ursula walked into the cells here, the women greeted her with a smile and sincere gratitude. They weren't the muscular and masculine women she was expecting but looked just like her. Perhaps less well-maintained and certainly sicklier and thinner, but still like any other German woman. Under different circumstances, they could have become friends. Not that Ursula even considered this idea, fraternizing was a severe offense that could get her into hot water.

Ursula's favorite time of the day was leisure hour because then she could stand outside, enjoy the sunshine, and forget where she was. She kept an eye on the prisoners and couldn't help but overhear their conversations.

Margit and Hilde were particularly close to where she was standing. "So why are you here?" the newcomer asked her cellmate.

Ursula perked up her ears. The official file said that Hilde Quedlin had been found guilty of high treason. But what exactly she'd done, the papers didn't say.

"I used to typewrite papers for my husband, and one day he

asked me to type some technical material in a very peculiar fashion," Hilde answered.

"Peculiar fashion – what do you mean by that?" Margit asked.

"Well, putting several sheets of paper on top of each other, including carbon paper to make a copy. I didn't think anything of it at that time, except that it was peculiar."

"And then?"

Ursula moved a few steps, feigning disinterest, but staying close enough to eavesdrop.

"Those papers were technical blueprints from his work – radio transmission devices for the *Wehrmacht* – and he gave them to our enemies. I had already forgotten about it, but then he got arrested, and I as well." Hilde sighed, a depressed expression sinking over her face and her whole countenance. "The Gestapo thought I was involved."

Ursula couldn't help but press a hand over her mouth. There were so many rumors about what happened in Gestapo headquarters, and she didn't dare to imagine that some of those things had happened to the petite, friendly woman standing in front of her.

"You received a death sentence for typing something?" Margit's brown eyes glared, she stomped her foot and shouted, "That's so unjust!"

Ursula closed the distance to the two women, instinctively grabbing her baton in her right hand, and called her to order, "Prisoner Staufer. No shouting and stomping."

Margit looked at her like a frightened rabbit and nodded with wide eyes, while Hilde put a hand on her arm and addressed Ursula in a calm voice, "Sorry, Frau Hermann. It won't happen again."

Ursula nodded and removed her hand from the baton tied to her waist.

"Take better care, or I will have to report you to the director." Ursula felt the queasiness rising in her stomach. Margit Staufer's anger was understandable. She had wanted to shout out too upon hearing Hilde Quedlin's words. But rules were rules and had to be obeyed.

If people started to question the wisdom of the Government to do the right things, anarchy would soon reign in this country. *And how would that be any worse than it is now?* a pesky voice in her head asked. *Aren't people supposed to do the right thing for their country, even if it was the wrong thing according to Hitler?*

Ursula cast her eyes to the ground, shocked to the core by her own blasphemous thoughts. She was grateful for the sound of the bell announcing the end of leisure time. Questioning the rules was the beginning of the end. Or was it?

Days turned into weeks, and with every personal story Ursula came to know, her faith in the infallibility of the Führer and the Party was hacked away blow by blow. Even though she repeatedly reassured herself that the Government knew best, she had to acknowledge that most of the prisoners in Plötzensee didn't deserve to die. They weren't murderers or robbers; they had spoken out of line, handed out anti-Nazi leaflets, or hidden Jews from persecution.

Hannelore, a sixteen-year-old girl the same age as Lotte, arrived at the prison for hiding her Jewish stepbrother. Ultimately, the police had found him and dragged him away at the same time as arresting her for subversive acts against the government.

Tears prickled in Ursula's eyes as she saw the hopeless child riddled with fear and guilt. She smiled at Hannelore and – against all rules – spoke a few sentences of encouragement to her. The smile she received in response was like a cherished gift. From then on, Ursula found small ways to help the condemned prisoners. Smuggling secret messages out of prison. Letting them smuggle money inside. Extending visiting hours for a few precious minutes. Or with just a few words of encouragement.

With every little deed, Ursula's step became brisker and her smile broader. It was pure joy to see how much these women appreciated her tiny gestures of kindness.

On a particularly quiet day at the prison, Ursula entered the small concrete rooms with rickety metal bunks that housed Hilde and Margit to deliver a package from Margit's parents.

Hilde Quedlin looked particularly sad this day, and Ursula couldn't resist telling her highly classified information she'd received from her superior the day before. "It's not official yet, but it seems women aren't executed anymore."

The prisoner's face lit up like a chandelier. "That's good news, isn't it? After all, I might get to raise my children…"

Ursula could tell that the poor woman was holding back her tears, and she backed out of the cell without a further word to give her some privacy. But as she was about to close the door, a soft voice said, "Wait."

Ursula glanced back. "Yes?"

"You know, Frau Hermann, I really appreciate your kindness. We all do," Hilde said, and Margit nodded in agreement.

"It's nothing, really." Ursula shook her head as a small sense of pride and achievement spread through her chest.

"It is. In here, even a single word of encouragement means the world. You're an angel sent from heaven to help us through these difficult times."

"Our Blonde Angel," Margit said with the irreverence of youth, but Ursula chose not to chide her and left without a further word. Deep inside her heart, she was proud of her new nickname.

That day she came home in the morning after a tiring night shift to find her sister Anna getting ready for work. For the past days, they'd communicated via notes left on the kitchen table because they usually missed each other by an hour or two.

"Morning, Anna," Ursula said and tossed her handbag on the kitchen table.

Anna cocked her head and grinned. "What's going on with you? Shouldn't you be less...energetic?"

Ursula poured herself some herb tea and sat at the table to tell her sister about her newfound mission. "You know, it's such a good feeling to bring comfort, even in such a small way. I believe I have found a purpose in my work: to care for these women when the rest of the world has stopped caring."

"Oh...oh..." Anna teased. "This is my older sister. Always watching over someone."

Ursula scowled at her.

"But I'm proud of you. If we all fight for a bit of humanity amidst the darkness of this crazy war, then not all is lost." Anna embraced her sister and then said, "Sorry, sis, but I have to run, or I'll be late for work."

CHAPTER 5

By the end of May, Berlin was in full bloom. Chestnut trees boasted their white and pink blossoms, making passers-by smile. It was as if nature itself had decided to defy the horrors of war and replace gray rubble caused by the continual bombing with colorful flowers.

Ursula walked to her apartment, carrying two bags filled with her and Anna's rations for the week. She glanced up at the clear blue sky and wondered whether the war had been nothing but a bad dream. A nightmare that had disappeared with the spring sun casting a golden light along every surface it touched while warming the hearts of everyone in the capital.

Perhaps this magnificent day was a harbinger of happier days after the war in a not so distant future. How much she wished it would be true!

She put down the heavy bags of groceries and fumbled with the keys to the apartment door when Frau Weber, the nosy next-door neighbor, opened her door and peeked outside. "Oh, there you are, Ursula, I was waiting for you."

"*Guten Tag*, Frau Weber," Ursula said in her friendliest voice despite groaning inwardly. Now, Frau Weber would inevitably start with an avalanche of questions about Ursula's and her family's lives.

"The mailman came earlier today and left a telegram for you." Frau Weber held the official-looking envelope in her hand.

Ursula's heart thundered in her throat, and her knees were about to give out. A telegram. That slip of paper could hold news either terrific or awful. Never in between.

"Thank you," she managed to say and took the envelope with trembling fingers from her neighbor's hands. She wouldn't give Frau Weber the satisfaction of witnessing her opening it. She shoved the telegram into the bag with the groceries. Then she opened her door and stepped inside, where she leaned against the closed door.

The temptation was overwhelming, but Ursula decided to first put the groceries away. Then she flopped onto her bed and ripped the envelope open.

Frau Ursula Hermann,

We are sorry to inform you that your husband, Andreas Hermann, has been killed in the line of duty. His commanding officer sends you his deepest sympathies...

The rest of the words blurred with the tears streaming down her cheeks. In a matter of seconds, the telegram had wiped out the sunshine, and the room sat in cold and shadows. *Andreas is dead. Dead!* With him, all her hopes for a better future had disappeared. She bawled at the loss – at their beautiful past and the common future they wouldn't have. Her dreams dissolved with every shed tear, leaving nothing but a big, glaring hole in her heart.

When she'd used up all her tears, the thought occurred to her that not only was she now a widow, but a widow who had never enjoyed more than a passionate kiss with her husband. She and Andreas had never even been together as husband and wife. What if she would never love another man? Experience the joys of a family? Have children? Suddenly, she understood Anna's being upset about the lack of men. It was shrouded in the fear of... *what if there were none left when this awful war ended?*

Ursula spent the rest of the day like a zombie. She did not eat, nor did she cry. She wandered from room to room, sitting in different chairs trying to escape the internal discomfort. But the emptiness inside her only grew bigger with every passing minute. When Anna came home, Ursula handed her the telegram without a word.

Her sister read it and then held Ursula in a silent embrace. There was nothing to say, no bright side to consider, no comforting words to utter.

The next morning, Ursula covered her puffy eyes with makeup and returned to work. Despite her best efforts to hide her sobbing grief, one look into the concerned faces of the prisoners was enough to know they saw right through her strained smile. It would have been absolutely inappropriate for them to ask, but their apparently offhanded comments of compassion spoke for themselves.

When she couldn't keep her grief to herself anymore, she sought out the Catholic priest who worked at the prison, bringing moral support and consolation to all the inmates, independent of their faith or nationality. She waited until he returned to his small office before she approached him.

"Pfarrer Bernau, may I speak with you?" Ursula asked him nervously. It was the first time she had engaged in a private conversation with him.

"Of course, my dear. Come in." Pfarrer Bernau was a gaunt man in his late forties with warm, brown eyes.

Ursula sat opposite him, looking down at her hands, which curled and shifted awkwardly in her lap. The priest didn't rush her, nor did he speak. But somehow, he managed to make the silence a comfortable one, and after several minutes, Ursula had gathered the strength to raise her voice.

"Father, I...my...I had to talk to someone. My husband has died – is dead. I don't really know what I came for, there's nothing you can do..." she said quietly, fighting her tears and glancing at the wedding band she stubbornly continued to wear.

"I'm so sorry to hear that, my child, it's a terrible loss. You are right, I cannot change this for you, but I am here to listen whenever you need someone to talk to." The priest's soft voice melted the carefully built walls around her grief. Ursula inhaled deeply, unable to speak as waves of emotion racked her body. The room was silent save for her quiet sobs. When she felt the priest's big hand on her own, she looked up into his kind brown eyes and suddenly felt silly.

This man had seen so much suffering. He'd accompanied hundreds of prisoners during their last hours, and now, here she was whining at the death of her husband in combat.

"I'm sorry," she whispered.

"Don't be sorry. Every suffering is unique and deserves to be heard. You have loved your husband and losing him is a harsh test that God has put upon you. But you must remain strong and cherish the good times you had with him. With time, your grief will heal," Pfarrer Bernau consoled her.

"But how can this be God's work? My husband died in this awful war, by the hand of another human. How can God even allow this?" Anger overtook her, and she jumped up to stomp her foot. "It's so unjust! Why Andreas? Why me? We have done nothing to deserve this!" She slumped back onto her chair, half ashamed at her outburst, but also strangely liberated.

"Bad things do happen to good people. It is not God's wish to hurt us humans, but he gave us free will and not everyone uses it wisely. You and your husband got caught up in the cogwheel of much greater events, and I'm truly sorry for you. Those who did wrong will pay for it in the beyond. Don't let yourself become embittered, but seek out ways to help and protect those still in this world."

Ursula pondered his words, not exactly sure what he wanted her to do, or if he had even suggested she do anything. But before she could ask a question, she heard a knock on the door.

After another glance at her face, the priest said, "Now go, my child. And remember, I'm here to listen whenever you feel the need."

"Thank you." Ursula nodded and left, giving way to one of the prisoners. On her way back to the women's wing, she passed through one of the men's wings. The same gray concrete floor, the same thick brick walls with gray metal doors with the barred observation holes, but somehow, the atmosphere was different.

The barely restrained anger hung like mist in the air, and loud voices wafted from within the cells to her ears. Ursula didn't mean to listen, but when she heard Pfarrer Bernau's name come up in a heated discussion, she inadvertently slowed down her steps and strained her ears.

"...the priest really has to be more careful. He should know that not every prisoner is trustworthy," a male voice said.

"I agree. Enough snitches are willing to sell their own mother to the Gestapo in an attempt to save their miserable lives."

"How many times have we told him not to openly admit his disapproval of the current regime? To be more careful and watch his back..."

Ursula hastened her steps. What she heard was unbelievable. If it were true, Pfarrer Bernau could be the next in line for execution. Her stomach churned at the image of this kind and caring man walking up the steps to the guillotine, his hands bound behind his back. She shook her head to make the image disappear and pushed the conversation to the back of her mind.

She'd misunderstood it. It had been a snippet taken out of context. It couldn't be true.

CHAPTER 6

T he next morning, an unexpected letter arrived from
Lotte.

Dear Sisters,

You know how much I hate to write letters, but anything is better than one single minute of the boredom I must suffer. If this village moved any slower, we would be going back in time. I have started turning to watch leaves fall when I need a little stimulation.

Frankly, some warfare would break the monotony nicely. You can laugh all you want, but the air raid back home at least provided some excitement. If I don't leave this place very soon, you'll have to write on my gravestone: "She died of utter boredom whilst an exciting war was raging in the rest of the world."

My only diversion is Aunt Lydia's five children. But tell me, how long can you occupy yourself crawling around with toddlers? I feel like I'm forced onto the periphery while world-changing events are happening at home. I want to be part of the future and do my share – and by this, I don't mean some stupid and boring work the Government deems best.

You two know what I really want to do.

URSULA PUT the letter down as the icy hand of angst squeezed her heart. Lotte was the kind of girl who'd do something downright stupid without ever considering the consequences – like committing the futile act of resistance against the forces in power. With trembling hands, she picked up the letter again.

I DON'T WANT to be surrounded by cows and hills and silence anymore. I don't want to wipe snot from the noses of the children or scold them when they are too noisy. I hate every second I am here. This is not living – I have never had such a purposeless existence, including when I was an infant and did nothing but defecate.

URSULA GIGGLED at her sister's outburst of temper. It was as if the red-curled wildcat was standing in front of her, stomping her foot the way she did when she couldn't get her way.

A noise from the hallway distracted Ursula, and she looked up to see Anna standing in the door like a drowned rat. Instinctively, she looked out the window, but the thick blackout curtains prevented her from seeing outside.

"Raining hard?" she asked and laughed at Anna's pouty face.

"No, I thought I'd take a shower fully clothed. Saves me washing."

"Come on. Take off your wet clothes, and I'll make us tea. Then we can read Lotte's letter together." Ursula got up from the couch and entered the kitchen.

"Hey. You're joking, right? Lotte doesn't write letters. That would be the first in the two years she's been gone." Anna kicked off her shoes and coat and came after her sister.

"I'm afraid she's about to do something stupid," Ursula answered and pointed to the letter lying on the coffee table. "Be prepared for some entertaining melodrama."

Anna flopped onto the couch and read aloud:

DON'T GET ME WRONG. I'm grateful for the absence of air raids, despite my jokes.

Mutter has taken up sewing work for the farmers to earn money, and she tries to teach me sewing and other household tasks, unaware that I'm destined for greater things. My biggest accomplishment won't be an elegant appliqué on a god-forsaken pillow.

If I ever ponder the idea of becoming a housewife, will one of you please kill me first?

"HEAVENS, THAT'S SO LOTTE!" Ursula exclaimed, interrupting her sister's reading.

"Well, we never actually reckoned that Mutter would succeed in stamping her down, did we?" Anna said with a frown.

"I guess not. Our little sister burns with a fire that cannot be put out," Ursula agreed. "Read on."

Anna obeyed.

ON A BRIGHTER NOTE, I have finally made friends with another girl here. Irmhild is more intelligent than the rest, and she works at the town hall in the town where my secondary school is.

Through her, I may have found something useful I can do. I'm not *stupid enough to think I can change the world, but my actions can at least make a change for a few people.*

LOTS OF LOVE, *Lotte*

"NOW I'M REALLY WORRIED," Ursula said, trying to banish the odd sense of foreboding invading her soul.

"No, it's probably just talk. You know what she's like," Anna answered, but the clipped tone of her voice betrayed her true feelings.

"Should we call Mutter?" Ursula whispered.

"And tell her what? That Lotte has written a letter and wants to do something useful?"

Ursula gave her sister a fake scowl. "She'll get herself into serious trouble. I can just smell it."

"When has she ever kept herself out of trouble?" Anna laughed. "Do you remember that time a boy from her class told her that girls were inferior to boys, and she'd never be anything more than a housewife?"

"He never saw her fist coming," Ursula mused, but deep down she couldn't help feeling a little jealous. Lotte *truly* burnt with a never-ending fire. There was something infectious about her passion and unfailing enthusiasm for living and making things better. Her little sister possessed a kind of true bravery that very few did.

Ursula and Anna spent the rest of the day absorbed in household chores. Since their mother left for the country, they had come to appreciate the sheer quantity of things she had done to help them.

Certainly, they enjoyed the freedom away from Mutter's eagle eye. No longer did they share a room, or have to tidy immediately after making a mess. But it wasn't what they had dreamed of as teenagers – a life with no rules or curfews. Instead, they had to shop for groceries, cook, clean, and wash in addition to going to work every day.

CHAPTER 7

The months flew by in a blur, and summer flashed by before Ursula's eyes. Her work at the prison, though still a hindrance to her happiness, remained much more pleasant than before. Despite her feeble attempts to prevent it, Ursula had developed a bond with the female inmates.

She had cried tears of joy when Margit Staufer was released into freedom and tears of sadness when Hilde Quedlin was executed. It had been an unpleasant surprise for everyone at Plötzensee because Hilde had been the first woman to suffer this fate after the unofficial statement that women weren't executed anymore.

The tension in the cellblock had increased to a point where it was palpable, and every woman had been asking herself if she were next in line. Ursula's heart went out to them, but there wasn't much she could do. If she was openly friendly with these women, her own life would be in danger.

In the first week of September 1943, Ursula walked the familiar path from the bus station to Plötzensee in the evening twilight. The hot summer was giving way to warm days and chilly nights while the leaves on the trees started to turn yellow.

Ursula stifled a yawn and dragged her feet toward the prison entrance. She'd begrudgingly agreed to cover for a sick colleague and work all night shifts that week. After a forty-eight-hour weekend shift, tonight would be her third night shift in a row, and she could barely keep her eyes open.

"Good evening, Frau Hermann," Frau Schneider, who was on her way to leave the building, greeted her. "I'm sorry for making you work so much, but we're terribly short-staffed at the moment. In case of a problem, please report to Officer Mayer from the men's section."

"Yes, Frau Schneider." Ursula nodded to her superior. "I'm sure there won't be a problem. Nights are usually quiet around here."

The woman smiled. "I wouldn't leave if I didn't know I can count on you to keep it that way. Our inmates respect you."

Ursula shrugged and forced a smile before she walked toward the changing room. Frau Schneider was a good woman, but Ursula didn't dare to imagine how she'd react if she ever caught on to her prison nickname, *Blonde Angel.*

After her first inspection round, she settled into the staff room on the ground floor when all hell broke loose. She'd dismissed the earlier air raid warning sirens because the thick prison walls always gave her a sense of security.

Today, though, was different. A bomb hit nearby, and the crash reverberated throughout the building, shaking the floor she stood on. Dust flew up into the air and Ursula jumped into the corridor and ran down to the shelter, located in the basement of the old building.

She arrived to safety just as another bomb hit the building with a deafening sound. Officer Mayer counted the people in the shelter, and when he was sure all the guards had arrived safely, he locked the door from the inside. Everyone would have to stay until the all clear sign was given.

Even down in the basement, the walls trembled with the

impact of bomb after bomb. Ursula crouched in a corner, avoiding the gazes of the other fifteen-or-so guards. She feared she'd find her own terrible guilt etched on their faces.

They'd left the men and women behind bars to their fates. Locked up. Not allowed to find safety. She didn't know how long she listened to the dull thuds echoing around them, smelling the dust and smoke in the air while fearing for her life before she fell into a fitful sleep.

She woke many times throughout this hellish night, the terrified faces of the prisoners in their cells haunting her dreams. More than once, she was about to jump up and crash into the thick door, feeling the need to break out and help the men and women upstairs before they burned alive. But she knew from experience that she wouldn't even make it near the door before the other guards would throw her down and hold her still until her breakdown eased.

She'd seen it happen more than once in the *Hochbunker* near her house. Sometimes, people panicked, and all they wanted was to get out. But it was too dangerous to open the doors during an attack, and the hysterical person had to be silenced by any means. That sometimes included a well-targeted punch to their head.

Many, many hours later, the all-clear siren shrilled. Ursula woke with a start and stretched her stiff limbs. Then they left the basement to take stock of the damage to the prison building.

The air was still filled with dust and smoke. Much to Ursula's relief, the women's section was almost untouched. However, the main building of the prison presented a picture of utter devastation. Rubble wherever she looked. The building must have received several direct hits, and the ensuing fire had done the rest. Most of the cells were empty, the metal doors hanging idly on their hinges. Iron bars had been ripped like sticks of licorice and bricks had shattered into sand.

Ursula and the other guards entered the courtyard where

most of the terrified prisoners had gathered. She stared at the gaping hole in the wall of one of the cellblocks. Furthermore, the roof of the execution chamber was stripped, and the guillotine was torn from its base, damaged by fire.

Officer Mayer assigned the guards into pairs and tasked them to count prisoners and match numbers to names. Soon, they were joined by the incoming day shift, and within an hour, all the prisoners had been counted, recounted, and cramped into the remaining intact cells.

The prison director arrived, and judging by his worried face, there was a problem. After going through the lists of names again, the director finally gathered all the guards and announced that out of the three hundred plus prisoners, four were missing. Files of the four missing prisoners were passed around.

Ursula was too tired to even blink when she was paired with a robust man from the day shift to search for the fugitives. The premises were scrutinized inch by inch, but by the time the sun hung high in the sky, burning down mercilessly on the battered city, they still hadn't found even one of the missing prisoners.

"Have you seen that pile of rubble over there?" her partner asked.

"Yes. You think they got out there?" Ursula answered on another yawn. The idea of walking over to the far end of the courtyard and climbing over that rubble wasn't exactly inviting.

"Let's go and have a look."

Ursula sighed and trudged behind him to the pile of rubble scattered in front of the four-feet-thick brick and mortar wall surrounding the entire prison compound.

"Looks like there's a hole," her partner pointed out and glanced between Ursula and the crack in the wall. "You are small enough to crawl inside and have a look."

She groaned inwardly. That was just what she needed after the night of horror she'd just survived. But her partner was permanent staff and senior to her so naturally she had to do his bidding.

"Here, take my flashlight, and I'll help you climb over the pile of rubble," he added in a voice that didn't allow any objections.

With the help of her fellow guard, she reached the crack in the wall and squeezed inside. She couldn't distinguish anything except for eerie shadows, but her neck hair stood on end as if she was being observed. Her heart racing, she switched on the torch and gasped in the same moment when the beam exposed the terrified face of a man. Despite the fear on his face, he was a handsome man with thick dark hair, strong but pleasant features, and exceptional green eyes.

Recognition seeped into her brain. Tom Westlake. The file she'd been shown earlier stated he was an English airman. A spy.

She lowered the flashlight, but he held her gaze, locking eyes with her. She stilled, and a charge of electricity passed between them. Ursula had no idea what was happening and blinked the emotion away.

"Please. All I want is to live," the prisoner begged her.

She swallowed hard as the memories of Andreas and a happier time together with him swept over her. This man probably had a girlfriend, a mother, and a sister waiting for him at home, praying daily for his safe return.

His life now lay in her hands, as did the happiness of the innocent women who loved him. How could she be responsible for more suffering on this earth?

The prisoner clasped his hands together as if in prayer, and Ursula glanced one last time at him, giving a barely visible nod before she backed out of the hole in the wall.

"I can't see anyone," she yelled back at her waiting colleague. "The hole's a dead end. They must have escaped somewhere else."

CHAPTER 8

U rsula trudged to the administration building and entered the staff room without looking left or right. She wouldn't – no, she couldn't – look anyone in the eye, especially not her superior, Frau Schneider.

Oh God, what have I done? She not only let a prisoner escape. No, she had helped the enemy. This prisoner wasn't just anyone distributing leaflets. He was an English spy. An airman. His colleagues were responsible for reducing her beloved Berlin to nothing more than ruins and rubble. For killing hundreds and thousands.

Bile rose in her throat, and she had the strongest urge to vomit. Her actions were shameful on so many levels, and if she were found out, she'd be hanged. Rightly so. *I'm a disgrace to my Fatherland.*

Despite her exhaustion, guilt and remorse forced her to take a detour on the way to the bus station to pass by the crack in the wall from the outside. She didn't know what she expected to find and vacillated between hoping he was gone and hoping he'd still be there.

Ursula approached the spot with sweaty palms and found a

pile of rubble similar to the one on the other side of the wall. Her pulse ratcheted up as she noticed the crack and peeked inside. Empty. The only thing she could see was light coming through from the other side and something that seemed to be a reflection of the sun in one of the few remaining prison windows. *Thank God, he's gone.*

For a split second, fear grabbed at her. He might still linger, ready to attack her. Ursula closed her eyes and willed herself to breathe. He wouldn't gain anything from attacking her – and those intense green eyes hadn't carried a trace of violence. If – God forbid – she ever met him again, he wouldn't hurt her. She hoped.

After a few more moments, she released a deep sigh and opened her eyes to the bright sunlight. The whole ordeal was over. It had never happened. She never saw anyone. Nobody could prove the contrary.

But as she sat on the bus, seeing the destruction from last night's attack, anxiety pressed heavily on her lungs, making breathing difficult. She scrutinized every boarding passenger, praying it wouldn't be the escaped prisoner.

The short walk from the bus station to her building was like running the gauntlet. She jumped at every person walking by, as if they were about to shout, "Stop her! She helped the Englishman escape!"

Her comfortable calm had left the moment she stopped living by the rules. Even as she arrived home, this new agitation followed her inside. She remained preoccupied as she walked straight through into the kitchen, where Anna was making lunch.

"Hello, Ursula, I've been waiting for you," Anna greeted her before she turned around to look at her sister. She cocked her head. "Aren't you going to take off your jacket?"

Automatically, Ursula looked down, surprised to find herself fully adorned in her jacket and outdoor shoes. She started removing them but did not respond.

"What's bothering you, grumpy?" Anna's forehead creased into a slight frown.

"Nothing. I'm just tired," Ursula replied. It was only a half-lie. Her body was exhausted from lack of sleep, but her mind was abnormally alert, smelling danger everywhere.

"Don't act like I'm stupid. Ever since Andreas died, you haven't been the same. I'm not saying you should be..."

Ursula cast her sister a cold stare.

Anna stared right back. "Don't look at me like that. I'm worried about you. I know it's hard, but you can't collapse in on yourself. You hardly even smile anymore. Don't you remember what people used to say about your smile? How it could cheer anyone up, even in the darkest of times? I miss that." Anna took a step towards her sister, but Ursula backed away.

"It's not just Andreas..." Her composure was hanging by a thin thread, and she could feel tears spring to her eyes.

"Then what is it?" Anna asked, worry crossing her pretty features.

"I..." *Shut up, shut up*, her mind screamed, and she let out a long breath. "It's just that the night was hard. Don't worry about me. You're right, Anna, I'll try and be less withdrawn. It's just hard to build myself back up in times like these." Ursula forced her face into the very smile she was known for. "I'll go and get some sleep before my night shift starts."

"What about lunch?" Anna called after her, but Ursula had already closed her bedroom door and flopped onto the bed. She didn't bother to take off her clothes or close the curtains. She wouldn't be able to sleep anyway. How could anyone live with that constant fear stabbing her in the heart?

Exhaustion took over, and she dozed off, tossing and turning in bed, her dreams paralyzed by images of the prisoner as well as people surrounding her, calling her a traitor. A noise from the front door woke her, and Ursula sprang to a sitting position in her bed, her eyes glued to the door, fully expecting Gestapo officers to rush in to arrest her.

When nothing happened, she closed her eyes and forced herself to breathe. She grabbed the lamp from her nightstand as a weapon and carefully opened the bedroom door.

Nothing.

Except for a note on a ripped piece of paper, lying on the table.

URSULA,

I HAVE to leave for work and won't be back until late afternoon tomorrow. Please eat, and I hope we can talk some time this week. I'm truly worried about you.

LOVE ANNA

PS: I went grocery shopping, but you still have to get washing soap.

URSULA SIGHED, and her heartbeat slowly returned to normal. Anna regularly worked twenty-four-hour shifts at the hospital, and sometimes the two of them went for days without seeing each other. When Mutter had still been around, she'd never noticed, but now with only the two of them...a single tear of loneliness rolled down her cheek.

A glance at the clock told her she still had a few hours before she needed to leave for work, but sleep was out of the question. She decided to run a few errands. Walking in the sunshine would hopefully clear her head.

As she left the apartment, she heard the telltale click of her neighbor's door, as the woman *accidentally* left her apartment with two shopping bags the exact same moment as Ursula did.

"*Guten Tag*, Frau Weber," she greeted the elderly gray-haired woman.

"*Guten Tag*, Ursula. I didn't see you in the shelter last night and worried about your safety."

The hell you did. "Thank you for your concern, but I had to work and spent the night at the shelter over there," Ursula answered without going into details.

"Thank God. Now that your Mutter is in the country, I feel it is my task to keep an eye on you girls." Frau Weber paused for a moment and made to accompany Ursula down the stairs. "Is it true that the prison was hit severely?"

"Yes, but we managed to get everything back under control. I'm very sorry, Frau Weber, but I'm in a hurry to run some errands." Ursula itched to get away from that nosy woman, or she'd soon be involved in some lengthy gossip about any and all persons living in the building.

"You young girls are always in a hurry. Go...I'll see what meager rations I will get for my cards, and then I'll visit my sister who lives three blocks away. She's not good on her feet anymore."

Ursula cast her a smile and dashed away. At least Frau Weber wouldn't be accosting her a second time today. After completing her errands, Ursula walked aimlessly through the streets of Berlin until it was time to return home and get ready for work.

"Hello," a deep voice came from nowhere.

Its distinct accent made her heart race. Surely not... She swung around searching for the source of the voice. There was no one to be seen. Had she finally cracked under the pressure and lost her mind?

"Down here," it said again.

This time, Ursula located where the voice had come from and peered over the low bushes at the side of the road. Lying on the ground, clutching his leg, was the prisoner she'd let escape this morning.

Ursula's hand flew to her mouth, covering the gasp that escaped her. *How has he found me?* Rage boiled up in her. *More to the point, why did he have to find me?* Every second she stayed near him increased her chances of being caught and condemned as a traitor. He must know that.

But as she looked down at him, her heart softened. There was something in his eyes she couldn't resist. Vulnerability. Honesty. She swallowed and took a closer look at his injury. His prison uniform had a long cut on the upper thigh, exposing an ugly wound with a thick crust of dried blood. If she left, he was certain to be caught again and be killed.

His expression was slightly crazed, as though in a delirium and fever, but he stared firmly at her with pleading eyes. *Why does he trust me? Just because I was weak and saved him once doesn't mean I'll do it again. In fact, I won't.*

Ursula's mind screamed at her to run as fast as she could. But something about this man captivated her. No matter how much her mind commanded to escape, her body remained where it was.

"*Sprechen Sie Deutsch?*" she whispered, trying to look natural as she bent low over the bushes.

"*Ein bisschen.*"

With a deep sigh, Ursula looked down at the man. "Follow me. You understand?"

He nodded and wobbled onto his feet.

"Here – take my coat to cover your uniform."

The escaped prisoner took Ursula's jacket and hung it over his large frame.

"Do not talk to me and hide behind the trees whenever someone approaches," she instructed him, looking up and down the street. Thankfully, dusk was settling over the city, but it wasn't completely dark yet.

Ursula walked to her apartment building, never looking back, unable to control the shivers of fear racking her body. She walked slowly, perking her ears for his limping step behind. Twice, they encountered a passerby, and Ursula prayed that the other person didn't notice the legs of the man's uniform sticking out from under the bottom of her coat.

When they finally reached her building, Ursula opened the door for him to stumble inside. Judging by the pained expression on his pale, sweaty face, he was close to passing out from the physical strain.

"How are you holding up?" she asked him.

"Just grand." He gave her a crooked grin, but it never reached his eyes.

"I live on the third floor."

The grin transformed into plain shock. "Not sure if I can make it."

No, he wouldn't be able to make it. Ursula cast caution overboard and wrapped her arm around his trim waist to drag him up the stairs.

"Thank you," he murmured, clearly embarrassed that he needed assistance.

They reached the third floor after what seemed like an eternity, and Ursula's heart was hammering against her ribs. She scrambled to unlock the door and shoved him inside. The moment she closed the door behind them, she heard heavy steps coming up the stairs and frantically peeked through the peephole. It was Frau Weber, heavily burdened with two shopping bags.

CHAPTER 9

"Shush. We can't risk anyone hearing you," she whispered as the prisoner leaned against the wall and groaned. Her strict voice reminded her eerily of Mutter.

Ursula took her coat off him and helped him to hobble into her room and sit down on her bed.

"I'll have to clean your wound," she said and disappeared to get a wet rag. Although she was scared, a strange nervous excitement was taking over.

When she came back into the room, he'd taken off his prison trousers, and she gasped at the sight of his bare legs in nothing but his underwear.

"Sorry." He used the dirty trousers to cover up his midriff and cast her a weak but crooked grin. "Thanks again."

She didn't respond and bit her lip in an effort to concentrate on the task at hand. There was a good reason that she, unlike her sister, had not chosen to become a nurse. One glance at his gaping wound and her head whirled with dizziness. She squinted her eyes to see as little gory skin as possible and puffed out ragged breaths as she cleaned the wound.

Her stomach revolted, and she had to look aside for a

moment before she could continue. *What the hell have I gotten myself into? I wish Anna were here, or Mutter...* The thought of her mother was enough to send the blood rushing back into her head. If Mutter were here, she'd have more serious problems than fighting her discomfort at seeing gore.

"What's your name?" she asked to stir up a conversation and distract herself. She already knew his name, but what else could she ask an injured enemy prisoner on the run? *Nice to meet you, thanks for bombing my country by the way.*

"Flying Officer Tom Westlake," he answered, wincing as the rag touched his leg again.

"Ursula Hermann," she said without looking at him. She pressed her lips together and forced herself to finish cleaning the wound.

"Thank you, Frau Hermann. I'm sorry...I shouldn't have come to you, but I had nowhere else to go..." he said in surprisingly fluent German.

His eyes conveyed so much misery that she almost forgave him for getting her into this dangerous situation. He was just a man. A fellow human. Apart from the fact that he was born in another country and spoke another language, he was exactly like her. All he wanted was to stay alive. Like anyone around here. Feelings of grief overwhelmed her and tears shot into her eyes as she thought about Andreas, the husband she lost. Flying Officer Westlake's loved ones shouldn't suffer the same heartbreak. Not if she could prevent it.

"Shush. Don't talk," she said and covered him with a blanket. His face had taken on a sickly greenish sheen, and he looked even more vulnerable now as he leaned against the white linen.

"I'll bring you water and something to eat. Then I have to go to work. You must not leave this room or make any noise. It is vital that nobody suspects you're here. Do you understand, Herr Westlake?"

He nodded weakly, and by the time she returned with a glass

of water and some buns with ham and cheese, he'd already drifted off to sleep. Ursula left the provisions on the nightstand and tiptoed out of the room.

~

URSULA ARRIVED at the prison and went through her chores like a machine. The inmates were tense and talked in hushed whispers about the events of the night before. Normally, Ursula would have tried to ease the tension with a smile or a friendly word. But every time someone mentioned the four men who had escaped, she flinched. Guilt and remorse settled deep in her bones, and her logical brain tried to figure out why she'd helped Flying Officer Westlake. He was the enemy – responsible for killing thousands of her compatriots.

"Frau Hermann, a word, please?"

Ursula jumped at the voice of her superior. *They found out. I'm as good as dead.*

"Yes...Frau Schneider?" Ursula turned around and looked into the piercing eyes of her superior.

"I have observed you for a while now, and you are unusually agitated. Is something wrong?"

Ursula shook her head. "No."

"Is it because of the escaped prisoners?" Frau Schneider insisted.

God, yes. How does she know? "They haven't been found, have they?" Ursula managed to press out.

"I'm afraid not. Don't worry. Nobody will hold you responsible. It's the fault of those bloody Englishmen."

Ursula let out a breath. "*Danke,* Frau Schneider. It's just...last night, the destruction of the building, the escaped inmates, it's been a lot to handle. But..." she faked a confident smile, "I'll be fine. I just need a day or two."

"We are all high-strung with this awful war," Frau Schneider nodded and left.

"Frau Hermann, do you have a moment?" one of the women called after her.

"Yes?" Ursula walked over to her cell. Due to the destruction in the other part of the building, they had crammed six to ten prisoners in a cell that normally held two or three at most.

"My family must be frantic with sorrow. Could you post this for me so they know I'm safe?"

Ursula looked around to make sure nobody saw her, even though basically all of the guards smuggled things in and out of prison, even Frau Schneider. But appearances had to be kept up, and it was better not to be seen.

"Of course," she answered and took the letter and stamps the woman handed to her.

Then she continued her rounds and distributed parcels that had arrived from relatives for the prisoners. The prison administration welcomed those parcels, because without food from the outside, inmates would starve to death on the meager rations.

Today, it took much longer than usual, because most of the inmates had been relocated to different cells. But Ursula was grateful for the chaotic circumstances because it occupied her mind enough that she didn't think about the Englishman in her home.

At the end of a tiring night shift, she returned home with one single wish: to drop on her bed and sleep twelve hours straight. But a snoring noise reminded her of the fact that a handsome airman was sleeping in her room. She snuck inside to bring him fresh water and dried his sweaty forehead with a towel.

She wasn't sure whether he noticed or not because, although he gulped down the water, he didn't look at her and uttered unintelligible words in a language she assumed to be English.

After another glance at his pained face, she decided to sleep in the second bedroom that was now Anna's. As soon as she climbed into the huge bed that belonged to Mutter and Vater, Ursula drifted into a deep and dreamless sleep.

"Ursula, what are you doing in here?" someone shouted into her ear while shaking her shoulders.

"Let me sleep..." she murmured, rubbing her eyes groggily.

"Why are you sleeping in my bed?" the voice insisted.

Anna! It all came rushing back to her, and she sat up in bed, wide-awake.

"Don't be angry..." Ursula said and patted the place beside her.

Anna rolled her eyes but obeyed. "That's supposed to be my line. And it makes me worry that you're using it. What have you been up to?"

"Nothing. Please listen first and scold me later."

The frown on Anna's forehead intensified, but she nodded.

"Our prison was badly damaged during the air raid the night before, and four prisoners escaped."

"Go on..."

"Well... one of them is currently sleeping in my room–"

"What?" Anna all but shouted and leapt to her feet. "Are you out of your mind? There's an escaped prisoner in our home?"

"Shush...someone could hear you." Ursula tried to pacify her sister, but her interjection only served to agitate Anna more.

"That's insane. Dangerous. Suicidal even. Do I have to remind you what happens to people hiding criminals? You of all people should know!"

Of course Ursula knew. She witnessed it on a daily basis at work.

"I do," she murmured, fear prohibiting her from speaking loudly. "But...he was so vulnerable...I can't really explain it. I thought about Andreas and my horrible grief. Flying Officer Westlake is just a man. A human being like you and me. And he's sick. I had to help him, couldn't close my eyes and let him be murdered. I just couldn't..." Her voice broke, and she gave her sister a glance, pleading for understanding.

"Westlake?" Anna squinted her eyes, pressing her lips into a thin line. "His name is Westlake? And he's what? A soldier? Don't tell me he's an Englishman!"

Ursula buried her head in her hands, unable to look her sister into the eyes. "In fact, he is."

"You've brought the enemy into our home? One of those damned murderers? The same ones who drop their bombs on our city nearly every night?" Anna stopped pacing and stared at her sister with disbelief in her eyes. "Please tell me this is just a bad joke..."

"It's not. And I know everything you said. Don't you think I've told myself the same things?"

"He has to leave." Anna crossed her arms over her chest.

"I know, and I'm sorry, but he's badly injured and has a fever. I have no idea how to take care of him...but you do. You're a nurse." Ursula pleaded.

Anna stood motionless, staring down at her, but Ursula knew she'd got her sister thinking.

"Please."

"No way. He can rot in hell for all I'm concerned. He's the enemy. I'm not helping the enemy."

"You patch up patients on a daily basis so the Gestapo can torture them some more. Isn't it about time you actually *helped* someone with your nursing skills instead of setting them up for more suffering?" Ursula knew she was being unfair, but she needed her sister's help.

"That's totally different," Anna growled with a deadly stare.

"Ah, and how is this different? Haven't you pledged to help all patients?"

"Don't roll out the old chestnut of professional ethics," Anna answered, but she at least uncrossed her arms and took a step toward her sister.

"You and Lotte always told me to stand up for my beliefs. And you know what? You're right. It's about time we did something *morally* right." Ursula rose to her feet and put a hand on her sister's shoulder. "Please, Anna, I need your help."

"Fine. I'll have a look at him, but he disappears the moment his fever breaks," Anna said with a scowl before leaving the room to check up on her new patient. Ursula followed her to the bedroom next door.

Westlake was awake but in bad shape. He tried to conceal it with a grin but failed miserably. Ursula leaned against the doorframe watching her sister attend the patient. Despite Anna's cheerful smile, she noticed the underlying worry. She just wasn't sure whether her sister was worrying about the health of their patient or their safety.

"This has to be stitched," she said after inspecting his wound and then turned to her sister. "Ursula, can you please fetch my bag?"

A very pale man flinched despite his attempt to put on a brave face.

Ursula hurried to the other room to bring her sister the bag where she kept first aid material.

"You don't need me here, do you?" she asked in a low voice.

Anna recalled her sister's dislike for blood and grinned at her. "I guess not. I'd rather have only one patient."

"Thanks," Ursula said and grabbed the prisoner's dirty trousers to wash and mend them. He'd need something to wear when he left the bed. Just the thought of seeing him in nothing but his underpants again caused a peculiar feeling in her stomach. His legs were emaciated but still hinted at the strong muscles he must have possessed before being arrested. According to his file, he'd been captured more than six months ago and had spent quite a lot of time in the Gestapo's custody.

Ursula willed herself not to think about the things she'd heard and seen. Prisoners transferred from Prinz-Albrecht-Strasse rarely arrived in good shape.

Just as she was about to finish mending, Anna came out of the bedroom. "All done. He was quite brave, your Englishman."

"He isn't *my* Englishman," Ursula protested.

"Whatever you say. He barely winced when I had to stitch him up. I also made him calf packings against the fever and gave him Mutter's valerian drops to sleep. By the way, he said he's hungry, which is a good sign."

"Thank you, Anna. I'll bring him some food," Ursula said.

"Thank me when he's gone, and we're safe again. I'm going to sleep now."

CHAPTER 10

As Ursula arrived at the prison entrance, the gatekeeper, Herr Müller, instructed her to go straight to the main hall.

"Director's orders," he added.

"*Danke*, Herr Müller," she said, a rush of fear seeping through her body. Surely, the director could not know what she had done? Ursula crept toward the hall, dragging every step as long as possible, certain her ultimate demise was awaiting her.

But as she reached the hall, it was already filled with all prison guards on duty. A wave of relief washed over her. A few minutes later, the prison director entered the room and the murmurs stopped.

"Dear ladies and gentlemen, you may be wondering why I have summoned everyone today. I'm afraid it's not good news." The director looked from person to person.

Ursula seemed to notice an unusual tiredness in his voice. Certainly, the past days had taken a toll on him too. He'd always struck her as an upright man, and somehow, he'd managed to make Plötzensee a friendly place – compared to the other prisons she'd worked in.

"We have received a message from our Führer," the director continued in his booming voice, "While he is not laying blame on us for the escape of four prisoners due to the destruction caused by enemy shells, he is less than pleased with the slow progress in dealing with clemency appeals. The ministry of justice is now intent on speeding up executions. All clemency appeals will be decided upon within the next few days." The director paused, and the expression on his face didn't leave any doubt about the expected outcome.

"As most of you know, the execution chamber and the guillotine were severely damaged during the fire, meaning an alternative solution must be found. I will keep you informed. And..." the director paused and let his eyes wander, "I don't have to tell you how important it is not to let the prisoners know. The situation is bad enough as it is, we don't need the added tension. Heil Hitler!"

Everyone in the audience raised his right arm in salute, before turning to each other, anxious about what was to come.

Ursula noticed Pfarrer Bernau standing near the door with a solemn face.

"Good morning, Father," she greeted him.

"Good morning, my child," he said with a sigh. The announcement had clearly shaken him.

"I wish there was a way to help. This feels so wrong," Ursula murmured more to herself.

"Unfortunately, there is no way to help the poor souls in here. All we can do is extend our hand and help those still in freedom." Pfarrer Bernau looked intensely into her eyes, "It is our responsibility to help those who are innocent."

Did he actually ask me to resist the authorities? Surely not. But then Ursula remembered the discussion of two inmates about the priest's political opinions.

Ursula went through her shift pondering the meaning of Pfarrer Bernau's words and whether she'd done the right thing by rescuing Tom. In the light of the new developments, he would have been dead within a few days.

The responsibility lay heavy on her shoulders.

After her shift, she returned home and bumped into Frau Weber.

"Good evening Ursula," her neighbor greeted her as she slipped out her front door.

"Good evening, Frau Weber." Ursula groaned inwardly. *What does she want now?*

"Is your father on home leave?"

Ursula grabbed her handbag tighter as she tried to keep her face carefully neutral. "No, Frau Weber, unfortunately not. We haven't heard from him in a while."

"I could have sworn I heard a male voice in your apartment," the neighbor insisted.

"A man? In our place? You must have been mistaken, Frau Weber. We are honorable women." She shot her neighbor an indignant look and unlocked the door with trembling hands. *That woman will be the death of me.* She made a mental note to warn Officer Westlake to be even more careful and make no noise when he was alone in the apartment.

She peeked her head inside his room and watched him sleep. He'd turned and tossed last night, speaking in his delirium, but he now looked calm and peaceful. His face hadn't lost its boyish charm and his wicked smile…

Stop it.

Ursula turned on her heels and busied herself making dinner, raiding the pantry and switching on the gas stove. Then she dropped a glob of margarine into a hot cast-iron skillet. It danced inside the skillet, sizzling and sputtering as it melted while she sliced cooked potatoes from the day before. As they roasted and turned golden-brown, a delicious aroma filled the kitchen. She added pieces of ham – courtesy of Aunt Lydia – and Mutter's special seasoning to make *Bratkartoffeln*.

Several minutes later, she piled a big portion onto a plate and with a tray of food entered the bedroom currently occupied by Flying Officer Westlake. He blinked and sniffed. When his eyes opened, he greeted her with a genuine smile.

"Good evening, how are you feeling?" she asked with a shy smile.

"Much better. Your sister is a truly excellent nurse. My fever broke." He grinned at her. When she didn't respond, he added, "I will never be able to thank both of you enough for what you've done."

An awkward silence ensued. His English accent reminded her that he was the enemy in this awful war. Helping the enemy was punished draconically. But on the other hand, his charming grin warmed her heart.

"Is that food for me?" he broke the silence, licking his full lips.

"I made *Bratkartoffeln,* fried potatoes with ham. Are you hungry, Herr Westlake?"

"Like a wolf. That smells grand." Tom winced as he moved to sit upright.

"Wait, I'll help you." Ursula put the tray on the nightstand and stuffed another pillow behind his back. When she touched his shoulders, a confusing tingle ran through her body. He caught her hand, and his green eyes shimmered softly as he said, "Please sit with me, Frau Hermann, and we can talk."

Ursula nodded and sat on the edge of his bed, carefully avoiding touching him again as she handed him the tray with food.

"About that…you need to be more careful." She clasped her hands, not daring to look at him while he wolfed down the food. "My neighbor said she heard noises in here and a male voice."

His eyes widened, and he immediately looked contrite. "I'm sorry. I don't want to cause you trouble. I'll leave tonight."

Ursula turned her head to look at him. A wave of sorrow almost broke her heart. "No, you can't. With your injured leg and your prison uniform, you wouldn't get far."

"But here, I'm a potential problem for you and your sister," he insisted.

Ursula buried her head in her hands. "I know...but...I can't be responsible for your death. In the prison..." tears started rolling down her cheeks, and her breathing became forced, "...they...all...it's so awful..."

"Shush." She felt his hand on her shoulder as his deep voice tried to calm her down. "Everything will be fine–"

"Nothing will be fine!" She jumped up, only to fall back on the bed again, pressing her hands over her mouth. Then she took several breaths and whispered, "Hitler has complained about the slow process of the clemency appeals. They'll execute everyone with a death sentence within the next days."

He visibly tensed at her words. "I wish I could turn time back and somehow prevent this awful war from ever happening."

"That would be nice." Despite her agitation, Ursula had to smile. It was ridiculous, but somehow his presence gave her a feeling of safety – and boldness. The woman who'd never broken a rule in her life suddenly had the urge to prove to the world how strong she really was.

He emptied his plate and gulped down a glass of water. "That was the best food I've had in months. Any chance I'm already dead, and you're in fact an angel, Frau Hermann?"

Ursula giggled. "No. You are still very much alive, Herr Westlake, and I'm no angel either." She flushed bright red at the unintended double meaning and spluttered out more words. "Please, everyone calls me Ursula."

"Ursula it is, then." His lips twitched, and he cast her a wicked grin, "I guess it would only be fair if you called me Tom. After all, you've already seen me in my underwear." Judging by the twinkle in his eyes, he thoroughly enjoyed her embarrassment.

"Herr Westlake – I mean Tom." Ursula paused, not sure how to continue. "May I ask you a question?"

"Sure. That's why you're sitting here with me, to talk." His grin broadened.

"I, uh, read your file, the night you escaped. All the guards had to…" She trailed off, unsure how to finish.

"And now you want to know if I really am a spy?"

Heat rushed to Ursula's cheeks, no doubt coloring them a deep purple.

Tom, though, laughed out loud. "Gosh, with an accent like mine, Hitler would have to be barmy not to have shot me on the spot." He sobered and gave the abashed Ursula a reassuring look. "I am not a spy. I cannot, however, deny being British."

Ursula pushed her blonde waves behind her ears, not sure whether his confession was good or bad. What difference did it make if he was a spy or a simple airman? Wasn't it even worse if he'd been amongst those dreaded pilots dropping bombs on her country? Her head was starting to hurt with all those contradictory thoughts.

"So, what happened? How did you end up with a death sentence in Plötzensee?" she asked curiously.

"I'm a member of the RAF, the British air force. I was flying a mission over Germany when my aircraft was shot down. I managed to bail out but was caught by the police."

An icy hand grabbed at Ursula's heart. How many times had she cheered when anti-aircraft flak had hit an enemy aircraft and sent it tailspinning to the ground? She'd never thought of the crew as human beings. Men like Tom. Young men with their entire lives in front of them. With hopes and dreams. With family and friends that would have to mourn them. Like her Andreas.

More tears shot into her eyes as the inarguable severity of

war dawned on her. They weren't happy soldiers enthusiastically fighting for the Fatherland as the propaganda made believe. No, they were frightened young men doing everything to survive – even if that meant killing someone else.

"War makes murderers out of otherwise decent people," she murmured more to herself than to Tom, but judging by the pained expression on his face, he'd done his share of things he wasn't proud of.

"You're right. War is an ugly affair. You should probably hate me instead of helping me. But know this… I will be forever indebted to you, for you have saved my life…" His voice trailed off as he locked eyes with her, and she could see the same confusion in them that whirled in her head.

His words had caused an oddly intimate setting for two strangers, and Ursula scrambled up and said her goodbyes to him, her face still burning red.

She had barely closed the door to the bedroom when Anna appeared like a ghost, and Ursula jumped.

"You scared me," she breathed.

"Sorry. How is he?" Anna asked with a nod to the closed door.

"Much better. He offered to leave tonight, but I told him to rest and recover at least another day," Ursula replied.

"He can't stay here, Ursula. It's not safe. Not for him and not for us. The sooner he leaves, the better."

Ursula wrung her hands, knowing her sister spoke the truth. "I know we can't hide him here. Frau Weber is already suspicious. He needs to leave not only this building but the country." Ursula sighed. She had no idea about this kind of thing, but she'd never heard about an enemy airman sentenced to death for espionage strolling across the border into safety.

Anna wrapped her arms around her sister. "Sleep on it. We'll think of something tomorrow. I have to leave for night shift."

"Take care," Ursula called after her sister before she went to bed.

CHAPTER 11

The next morning, Ursula felt like she'd been run over by a truck. Images of executions had invaded her dreams. She left the building in the wee hours of the morning, after warning Tom once again to be absolutely silent when neither she nor Anna were at home. Thankfully, Frau Weber from next door was still asleep, and Ursula reached the street without further inquisition.

At the prison, life – or rather death – had run its course. Ursula found a vastly decreased lot of distraught prisoners trying to forget the terrible things that had happened during the night. She looked into exhausted faces filled with horror, grief, or apathy.

Even her colleagues from the night shift stood on wobbly legs and hurried to change into their civilian clothes as if this would separate them from their haunting memories. The silence, interrupted only by involuntary groans and hushed whispers, was disturbing. Nobody was able to look another person in the eye as they struggled to get away from the eerie shadows looming over Plötzensee.

Ursula didn't dare ask.

It wasn't until she saw Pfarrer Bernau that she grasped the enormity of what had occurred. The warm shine in the priest's eyes had dimmed, and the corners of his mouth drooped as he approached her with slumped shoulders.

"The mass executions have started," he sighed. The utter desolation in his eyes sent shudders down Ursula's spine.

"Oh God. Here? How?" Ursula couldn't wrap her head around the priest's words. She didn't actually want to know, had preferred to stay blessedly oblivious, but the words tumbled out of her mouth before she could prevent it.

"It was awful. All the prisoners were gathered in the courtyard. Throughout the night, row after row of men were called into the execution chamber in groups of eight…to be hanged."

"Hanged?" Ursula's hand flew to her throat. Hanging was slow and painful. It was a death method from the Middle Ages, used to draw shame upon the death candidate and his family.

"Yes, they couldn't repair the guillotine in time and opted for hanging as the method of choice. My colleague and I had our hands full and couldn't do more than utter a short prayer for each of the poor souls. May God forgive mankind." Pfarrer Bernau swayed and looked at her through bloodshot eyes. "One hundred eighty-six prisoners were killed last night. And it will continue tonight."

Dizziness attacked her, and Ursula steadied herself by leaning against the wall. There was nothing she could say or do, only wonder at the atrocities this war held in store for everyone.

The priest turned to leave without another word, and Ursula staggered to the women's wing. She did her rounds in silence, most of the prisoners sleeping through the day after standing at attention all night.

An eerie tension had settled over Plötzensee. Ursula wished her shift were over so she could flee this place, but at the same time, she wished it would never end – because, at the beginning of the night, the killing would start again.

On her last round of the day, she distributed the comparatively abundant rations to the remaining prisoners, unable to show her usual smile. But who would care for a smile on a day like this?

The last cell on the floor belonged to two women whose husbands had been convicted as traitors. As she approached it, she overheard them talking.

"Can you believe it? He's been doing this since before the war."

"I always knew that there was more to Pfarrer Bernau. He's a remarkable man."

Ursula perked up her ears.

"It's unbelievable, isn't it? Right under the Nazi's noses, he's been hiding Jews and smuggling them out of the country."

"I wish he could smuggle us out of this hellish place too."

"Don't be silly. This is one of the best-secured prisons, there's no way we could get out."

"Well, four prisoners got out."

"Certainly, but they'll find them soon enough. Nobody hides in Berlin without help. And who would help our enemies?"

Ursula stopped breathing. Her head whirled. Pfarrer Bernau was hiding Jews? What if...no...or maybe? A million thoughts raced through her head, and her excitement grew by the minute.

She finished her shift, changed into civilian clothes, then took the tram to the hospital where Anna was working.

Ursula hated hospitals. The distinctive smell always gave her the shivers. But in her haste to tell Anna about her epiphany, she didn't notice. She sprinted through the building to her sister's ward, drawing the disapproving glances of more than one nurse. She stopped at the glass door and waved wildly at her very surprised sister.

"What on earth are you doing here? Has something happened with…?" Anna asked in a hushed voice.

"I found the solution!" Ursula exclaimed, drawing more attention to them.

"Wait right here," Anna demanded and left to talk to her superior. When she returned, she said, "I've got five minutes. Come." She led her sister into a break room and closed the door. "Now spill it. But keep your voice down."

"I know how we can save Tom. The priest at the prison…" Ursula paused, looking nervously around, and lowering her voice to barely a whisper, "he has been helping Jews escape for years."

"Are you serious?" Despite Anna's attempt to keep her voice down, it seemed to echo off the walls of the tiny room.

"Pretty much, yes."

"But who says that this priest will help us? After all, your Englishman is not a Jew. He's the enemy." Anna wrinkled her forehead.

"It's worth a shot. In fact, it may be the only chance to get him out of the country," Ursula whispered.

"Then ask him." Anna embraced her sister, and for a short moment, Ursula was certain everything would turn out fine.

"I will. See you tonight."

The two sisters left the break room, and Anna accompanied her to the entrance door of the hospital.

"I love you." Ursula kissed her sister on the cheek. "And I'll never forget what you did."

"You just be careful, all right?"

Ursula nodded and felt a flush rising in her cheeks under the scrutiny of her younger sister. She knew what Anna was thinking. She was worried herself. Tom had begun dominating her thoughts, and what she was feeling was much more than worry or compassion. His black humor made her laugh. His presence gave her a feeling of safety. His charming smile turned her insides to mush. And the joyful tone of his voice when he was teasing her sent heat to places it should not.

It was mutual too – the way he looked at her when he thought she didn't notice – the cheerful expression on his face every time she returned home.

"I'm not blind, you know." Anna said.

"What are you talking about?" Ursula hedged.

"You like him. The Englishman."

"What? No, I..."

"It is pointless to deny it, sister. A part of me even understands. He's handsome, good-mannered, and makes you laugh. You haven't had much to laugh about this year. But he's still the enemy. There's no future for the two of you. He will never be safe in this country, and you won't be welcome in his."

"But Anna–"

"No buts, you have to be reasonable." Anna gave a short laugh, "Can you believe it's me telling you this? All our lives it was the other way around." Anna wrapped her arms around her sister. "I'm just worried about you. Promise you won't get attached to him?"

"I promise." It was a lie. She already liked Tom a lot more than was good for anyone involved.

CHAPTER 12

The next day, Ursula went to visit Pfarrer Bernau in his parish. She was still pondering her conversation with Anna from the day before. As much as she wanted to convince herself that Anna's warnings were pulled out of thin air, she knew better. Her – totally inappropriate – feelings for Tom were growing, which put her in an awkward position. Not only because he was an escaped prisoner, but also because of her sense of duty towards Andreas, who hadn't been gone for more than three months. She was betraying so many people in such a variety of ways, all for the attraction she felt for him.

The small church was a relatively new and plain building, unlike the ostentatious Berlin Cathedral that was reminiscent of the glorious times in the fifteenth and sixteenth centuries.

The plain transparent altar windows, probably replacements for damaged stained glass, let plenty of sunlight inside. But despite the light and the warm air outside, she wrapped her scarf tighter around her shoulders.

Apart from two elderly women praying in the first bench, the church was empty. Ursula looked around, trying to find Pfarrer Bernau. He might not even be here. She could have waited for him at the prison but was too anxious to discuss such delicate matters at her workplace.

A sign at the entrance to the sacristy told her he was hearing confessions. Ursula turned around and noticed the confessional booth on the left side of the nave. She grabbed her scarf tighter and walked over to the wooden booth. As soon as an elderly lady vacated the penitent's seat with a rosary in her hands, Ursula slipped inside and knelt down. Her heart was hammering against her chest.

"Bless me, Father, for I have sinned," she said with a trembling voice.

"Don't be afraid to confess. God forgives those who repent." Ursula recognized the warm and caring voice of Pfarrer Bernau. She clasped her hands together. This was a lot more enervating than she had expected. "Please continue, my child."

"I found a man who is wanted by the authorities," Ursula whispered. "He was injured, and I couldn't leave him to die, so I hid him in my home. Only now I fear someone will find out, and I will be condemned too. I need to find a way to get him to a safe place."

It was a few seconds before the priest responded as if he were contemplating her words. "That is a very unusual sin. May I ask your name, please?"

"Err, it's Hermann. Ursula Hermann." Her feet wanted to dart out, but she forced herself to stay kneeling in the confessional booth.

"Yes, I thought as much." The seconds dragged on without a sound to be heard. Ursula clasped her hands upon the wooden board beneath the screen, holding on for dear life. "Can you be trusted?"

What a question. Here she was, confessing to one of the deadly sins in the Party's book and he asked her whether *she* was trustworthy.

"Yes, of course!" Ursula responded, nodding her head in emphasis.

"I would be interested in meeting this man. But it needs to be done very discreetly, do you understand?"

Ursula nodded, before realizing that he couldn't see her. "Yes."

She gave him her address, and he promised to visit in the evening to discuss further details. Ursula spent the day at work vacillating between hope, fear, and excitement. After her shift, she hurried back home and arrived at her building at the same time as the priest.

They walked up to the third floor side by side, talking about the weather and the difficulties in securing enough rations. When Ursula stopped to unlock her door, she heard the familiar click of Frau Weber's peephole, and seconds later, the neighbor's door opened.

"Guten Abend, Ursula," the plump woman on the cusp of old age greeted her, unashamedly eyeballing the priest. "Who is coming to visit?"

"I'm Pfarrer Bernau," answered the priest, saving Ursula from having to answer. "I'm here to discuss the details for holding a memorial service for Frau Hermann's late husband."

"Really? He's been gone an awfully long time," the neighbor said, apparently not convinced.

"Frau..." Pfarrer Bernau searched the door plate for her name, "Weber. There is no fixed time to grieve. Everyone mourns in a different way."

"It's just that strange things are going on behind that door. I could have sworn I heard a male voice the other day." The suspicion in Frau Weber's voice sent chills down Ursula's spine.

"Thank you for being vigilant, Frau Weber, but I'm sure there is no need to worry." He turned to Ursula. "Or is there, Frau Hermann?"

She lifted her chin. "No. My sister and I are honorable

women, we wouldn't invite a man into our place." The lie came so naturally to her lips, Ursula surprised herself.

The neighbor shot her a doubtful glance, but returned to her own apartment and locked the door.

Ursula fumbled with the keys for what seemed like hours before she finally pushed her door open. Pfarrer Bernau followed her through the apartment, and she knocked on Tom's door.

"Enter," a soft voice said. Tom was sitting at the small desk and looked up from the letter he was writing with his usual bright smile. But the charming smile was replaced by an expression of alarm the instant he saw the man behind Ursula. Within a split-second, he'd changed from the kind man to a dangerous panther on the prowl.

Ursula actually liked that trait of his, as it showed how much he was ready to take control of the situation. A warm feeling seeped into her body. It had been such a long time since she'd been able to lean on another person. For more than eight months, she and Anna had been on their own.

"It's all right," she assured him and stepped aside to let the priest enter the room. "This is Pfarrer Bernau."

Tom's face showed a multitude of expressions. Shock. Disbelief. Relaxation.

Pfarrer Bernau's face mirrored the same emotions. Then he stepped forward and extended his hand. "Aren't you the English airman who was accused of espionage?"

"Yes. Flying Officer Tom Westlake. I wanted to thank you. Our conversation in the prison gave me renewed hope and strength. Although I never would have expected this..." Tom made a grand gesture of pointing at the room and the persons present.

"Me neither." The priest showed a half smile. "It's rare enough for a prisoner to escape, but this? God must have great plans for you."

Neither Tom nor Ursula was particularly religious, and they both cast their eyes to the floor.

"Pfarrer Bernau is here because he may be able to help you." Ursula kept staring downwards as she uttered the words. She'd been silent for so many years, hadn't ever opposed a rule decreed by the Nazis. She'd never questioned the rightness of Hitler's doings, and the very thought of working against her country caused her stomach to revolt.

Her entire belief system had been shattered, and she longed for moral guidance. If breaking the law could be *right*, what was *wrong*? Who decided what was allowed and what wasn't? Who was the enemy, if her own government did things as heinous as the Nazis were doing?

Ursula wished someone, anyone, would tell her what to do. But looking into the eyes of Tom and Pfarrer Bernau, she realized that it was her decision alone to decide what was the right thing to do. It was somehow liberating, but also incredibly scary.

"Is that true?" Tom's hopeful voice stopped her train of thought. His face lit up, and she could read in it his hope and his desire to live. She admired the way he pushed his lower jaw forward, as it showed his unwavering determination.

"I may help, but your case is quite different to what I am used to. We have set up a network of people willing to hide German Jews until we have found a way for them to escape, but you...there aren't many people willing to help an Englishman. Every family has lost a member or a friend in this awful war, and emotions are running high." The priest looked pointedly at the blackout curtains. "And your compatriots remind us almost every night about the consequences of war."

"I understand." Tom ran a hand through his dark hair. "You are right. Your compatriots have every reason to hate me. I love flying, and I'm proud to be a member of the Royal Air Force. I never hesitated one moment to join up and fight for my country. Although I certainly don't enjoy killing people…" He paused a moment, and his gaze became empty. Ursula thought she saw a trace of pain – remorse? – but it was washed over in an instant. "This is war. There's no real choice. I, and so many others, couldn't let Hitler trample over our country, subduing our people like he has done with so many others."

Silence penetrated the room, as they each hung onto their own thoughts. War really was a dirty affair, and nobody would come out unscathed. Not the winners and certainly not the losers.

Pfarrer Bernau broke the silence first. "I will see what I can do. There might be a way to get you out of the country, but there are no guarantees. It will be a dangerous and strenuous undertaking. Are you willing to go through with it?"

Tom nodded. "I'll do anything it takes to get back home." His eyes lingered a moment on Ursula, and she felt herself blush. "It's in everyone's best interests that I leave this place as soon as possible."

"Not so fast, my son. You need to keep your feet still and lie low for a few more days until I have arranged the details and organized papers for you," Pfarrer Bernau said and produced a camera from his bag. "Look straight into the camera and don't smile."

Tom did as he was told, and minutes later, the priest bid his goodbyes.

Ursula showed him to the door. "Thank you, Father."

"Don't contact me, except in an emergency, and never in the prison. You understand?"

Ursula nodded.

"And one more thing, that neighbor of yours might cause a problem. Don't give her any reason to be suspicious."

Ursula sighed. The nosy Frau Weber had caused more than one problem in the past years.

CHAPTER 13

A couple of days later, the phone rang, and Ursula stared at the black instrument with surprise. It hardly ever rang.

"Ursula Hermann," she said into the earpiece.

"This is your mother."

Ursula almost dropped the receiver. Mutter hadn't called a single time since she left with Lotte for the countryside. She always said the cost of a long-distance call was much too high, and the money could better be spent elsewhere. What had changed her mind?

"Are you alright, Mutter?" Ursula asked and put her finger to her lips as she saw Tom coming out of his room.

"I am fine, thank you. How are you and Anna? We have heard troubling news about the Englishman–" Ursula paled and dropped the receiver to her lap. She struggled to put it to her ear again. "Ursula? Are you still there? What was that noise?"

"Sorry, Mutter, but I clumsily dropped the earpiece," Ursula answered for lack of a better response.

Her mother sighed into the phone. "I hope you didn't break anything. But that confirms me in my decision."

"What decision?" Ursula had difficulties concentrating on

the conversation as part of her mind was occupied as it frantically searched for clues to how her mother could have gotten news about Tom.

"To return to Berlin."

"You want to come home?"

"Yes. Home. To make sure everything is in order with you and Anna."

"We are fine," Ursula protested weakly.

"Well, as I said, we have heard so much troubling news about the Englishman intensifying his attacks over Berlin, I'm worried about my daughters."

Ursula wanted to jump up and embrace the world, until she remembered that her mother wanted to come *home*. To the same place her daughters were hiding one of those hated Englishmen. "But what about Lotte?"

"Lotte is fine with my sister, and I have the impression you two need me more. Besides, my presence has done nothing to make her watch her step. At least she has made a friend with a girl from the next town and seems to be much happier now."

"But Mutter, you're much safer in the countryside." Ursula tried in vain to keep the panic out of her voice. She could see it in Tom's alarmed eyes as he poked his head into the living room again. She gestured for him to keep quiet, but he lingered in the doorframe, seemingly concerned about her state of agitation.

"Nonsense. I have to be where I am needed most," Mutter said with a voice that wouldn't brook any argument.

"But Mutter," Ursula insisted, "wouldn't Lotte miss you? It must be a great comfort to her having you near."

A chuckle came through the line. "You should know quite well that Lotte would be nothing but joyful at my leaving, one less pair of eyes to watch over her." Her mother paused for a moment and then startled Ursula with her question. "What are you hiding from me?"

"Nothing, Mutter," Ursula answered too fast and too determined.

"Well, in that case, I will make travel arrangements. Tell Anna for me, darling."

The phone line buzzed, and Ursula remained in a complete state of shock. For how long, she didn't know. A hand touched her shoulder, and she spun around to look into Tom's green eyes, filled with worry.

"I didn't mean to listen, but you sounded so upset. Bad news?" His soft voice eased the tension in her body, and she had the urge to lean against him, to borrow his strength and forget all her sorrows in his embrace.

She took a step away from him. "Yes and no. That was my mother, she's returning to Berlin tomorrow night."

Tom looked slightly puzzled, and Ursula explained. "She lives here, and she would never approve of a man in the house, enemy or friend."

"Oh." Understanding lit Tom's eyes. "In this case, I will disappear tonight. I don't want to cause you more trouble than I already have."

Ursula could see the fear in his eyes, because out there in his – although washed and mended – prisoner uniform, he wouldn't go undiscovered for long. She appreciated his generous offer to put himself at risk so she wouldn't get into hot water with her mother. But the thought of Tom in the hands of the Gestapo – she was sure that was what awaited him – tore her heart apart.

"No. No. I will ask Pfarrer Bernau first. Maybe he has an idea. Promise you will still be here when I return from work?"

"I promise," he said, putting two fingers across his heart.

For a moment, Ursula thought he'd kiss her, but that, of course, was just her imagination.

She turned on her heels and left to find Pfarrer Bernau. Once she arrived at the chapel, she strode straight in and knocked on the door of his private quarters. To Ursula's relief, the priest was home.

"Frau Hermann, what is the meaning of this unexpected visit?" Pfarrer Bernau said, worry etched into his face.

"Father, I'm sorry. But this is an emergency. My mother is coming back to Berlin. Tom – Flying Officer Westlake has to disappear tonight."

Pfarrer Bernau furrowed his brows. "That is problematic indeed. There's no way to speed up his papers or the escape route. Those things take time and dedication." He looked at her with his warm brown eyes. "What if your mother learns about him?"

"No." Ursula shook her head violently. "She would never allow a man in our home. Not a German and much less an Englishman."

"We must find an alternative solution then, somewhere he can hide for a few more days. When is your mother due to arrive?"

"It depends on the train connection, but she might arrive as early as tomorrow night, or the day after."

"Then the transfer has to happen tonight. That doesn't give us much time." The priest turned to look out the window. "Unfortunately, he can't come here as I often have police visiting the Mass. There must be some place where nobody will find him."

"In the allotments." Ursula leapt up, her blonde waves bouncing around her head. "We have a tiny shed there and used to go a lot, but since the attacks on the nearby industrial compound, we've been warned it's unsafe. There's a strict curfew in place, and people aren't allowed to spend the night."

Pfarrer Bernau turned around. "That will do. It's only for a few days. But he'll need civilian clothes." The priest looked down his lanky frame. "I'm afraid Flying Officer Westlake won't fit into mine. Can you arrange for something?"

Ursula swallowed. "I will."

Tom was of a far broader stature than her father or her brother, Richard. It was out of the question that he could borrow their clothes. Andreas, though, had been about the same size as Tom, with blonde hair and blue eyes, in contrast to Tom's dark hair and emerald green eyes. Their smiles were strikingly similar and also the way they made her feel. It wasn't fair to Andreas. Nor was it to his mother whom she had to visit today.

"On second thought, take this." Pfarrer Bernau handed her a black soutane as she was about to leave, "Have him wear it over the civilian clothes when you're going to the allotments."

Ursula returned to work and arranged for a colleague to cover the last hour of her shift so she could leave early. Guilt slowed her pace as she trudged to the place where her mother-in-law lived. She hadn't visited her recently, for the simple reason that she couldn't stand the reminder of Andreas. Looking into the desolate eyes of the woman who'd lost both her husband and her son had been unbearable while Ursula wallowed in her own grief. Ursula knocked on the door.

"*Guten Tag*, Frau Hermann," Ursula greeted the older woman with the same blue eyes and blonde hair of Andreas. The distinct similarity made her stomach flip.

"Ursula..." Her mother-in-law reached out and pulled her inside the house into a warm embrace. "It's so good to see you. I was wondering when you would come by to see me. I understand it's hard after, well..." Frau Hermann's eyes began to glisten with tears.

"It's so hard. I miss him every day." Ursula looked down at her hands, fighting her own tears. "But, then, I missed him every day before too."

"Yes. That's true. This war is a terrible thing. It has stolen my husband and my only son. I do not know how I am going to recover, but you must feel the same. You two were such a nice couple. I hope one day you will find another man you care for as much."

Ursula was relieved that Frau Hermann chose that moment to blow her nose for she felt her face blush deeply.

"Frau Hermann, I have come to ask a favor." Lying had become a habit during the last days, and she barely flinched at her next words. "I have...nothing to remember Andreas by, for we never got to live together. I was wondering if you could permit me to have some of his clothes, some memorabilia for me to turn to when I feel alone."

Her mother-in-law's face softened. "Of course, Ursula. I haven't been able to give anything away. I know I should, because others need it so much, but I need the reminder of my son." She smiled kindly, and Ursula's heart sank a few inches. "Why don't you sit for a second, and I'll get some of his clothes for you."

Ursula breathed a sigh of relief as her mother-in-law rushed up the stairs. Guilt weighed heavily on her shoulders. Andreas had only been gone for three months, and here she was giving his clothes to another man. Her disturbing feelings for Tom didn't help to lessen the shame. She buried her head in her hands, her blonde waves falling like a veil over her face.

She wasn't only betraying Andreas with her infatuation for the Englishman, she'd lied, disrespected, and endangered everyone who was dear to her, including her Fatherland.

CHAPTER 14

"You look like a true German," Ursula said when Tom stepped out of his room dressed in Andreas' clothes.

"I could fool anyone, right?" He grinned and rose to his full, impressive height of six-one.

"As long as you don't open your mouth," Ursula giggled nervously.

Tom put on a mock offended face. "You want to imply my German is bad? That's not nice."

"Well, your German is surprisingly good, but your accent…" She imitated the peculiar way he pronounced the German words and giggled again. Her nerves were strung tight. Soon, the most dangerous part yet would begin, actually walking outside on the streets with him.

She handed him the black soutane, praying nobody would question the disguise. Then they waited together until the blaring radio from the apartment next door faded. Ursula could barely tolerate the rising tension as she listened intently for a sound.

"Frau Weber has gone to bed," she finally said. "Let's go."

Tom looked at her and must have noticed her trembling, because he took her hands into his. "Everything will be fine."

She nodded in silence and motioned for him to follow her. They snuck out of the apartment and scurried down the stairs like ephemeral ghosts. It was way past ten p.m., and the street lay empty in the dark, lit only by the dim moonlight.

Ursula knew the path to the allotments by heart, had walked the two miles thousands of times in her childhood, but never at night. After the Great War, Ursula's parents had applied for one of the allotments that sprang up throughout the city. Her mother had carefully tended the earth to grow some produce, but between household chores and work, Ursula and Anna had neglected the place and only worked the minimum to keep the fruit trees and bushes alive.

Tom fell in step beside her, following her lead without uttering a single word. They had almost reached the turnoff to the footpath into the allotments when her blood froze at the sound of a voice.

"Guten Abend, junge Frau."

Ursula spun around to look into the faces of two young officers clad in the black SS uniform. Her palms instantly became sweaty.

"Papers please," one of the SS men said. Both were sporting mustaches and couldn't be much older than twenty-five. Their guns poked out of their waistbands as if itching to be used. Ursula's heart was drumming so hard, she expected to hear it echo off the buildings surrounding them.

"Of course, one moment please," she said, making an effort to keep her voice stable. The officers stood waiting, one smoking a cigarette as Ursula reached into her handbag for her identification papers. Every time the man raised the tip of the cigarette to his lips, it made a gentle sucking noise, followed by a deep and slow exhalation. The distinct smell of nicotine wafted into her nostrils, subduing the smell of fear – a fear most everyone sensed when being confronted by the SS.

Ursula handed him her papers, waiting with bated breath. Out of the corner of her eyes, she noticed Tom tense. By now, she knew him well enough to know that beneath the priest's soutane, every single muscle had tightened, and he was alert like a panther on the prowl.

"It's rather late for such a beautiful woman to be out and about," the first one said with a charming grin.

"Yes, sir," she answered and caught a glimpse of Tom's scowling face.

"Can we escort you somewhere?" the young man asked, obviously attempting to flirt with her.

"Thank you, sir, I will be fine…" She followed the glance of the second officer over to Tom wearing the priest's habit. "My mother-in-law is in dire health, and I called for the priest to visit her."

It may not have been the wisest thing to say, but she hadn't been able to come up with a better explanation. Tom furrowed his brow in sorrow and raised his hand to the cross around his neck, murmuring some unintelligible words that sounded like a Latin prayer.

"Well, under these circumstances, Frau…" the SS man looked at her papers again, "…Hermann, we won't bother you further." He returned her papers and stepped back. "God bless you, Father."

As the SS officers walked away, Ursula staggered with a sudden wave of dizziness and Tom caught her arm.

"I almost died of fear," she admitted. "If they'd asked for your papers, it would have been over."

"Not without a fight," he said and held her elbow tighter. "But you're right, we were lucky. Come on, it's not safe here. We should get off the street or risk running into another patrol."

A few hundred yards down, they turned onto a gravel path

to the allotment garden complex. The moon slipped behind a cloud, and the increased darkness made orientation difficult.

"Watch your step," she whispered, "there's lots of weeds and roots covering the path."

During day the allotment area was like a huge patchwork quilt of deep browns and vibrant greens, made up of vegetable patches with small huts and sheds. She stopped in front of a wooden gate, taller than the height of a full-grown man, flanked by equally high Thuja hedges.

"This is your new home," she whispered with a grand gesture while she unlocked the gate and handed him the spare key.

"Smashing, and as impenetrable as Sleeping Beauty's hedge." Tom cast her a teasing grin.

As Ursula closed the gate again, a rusty squeak cut through the night, and she froze, listening to the darkness. Only when no sound was heard except for a barking dog in the distance did she dare breathe again. She motioned for Tom to follow her and crossed the small garden. In ten steps, they passed the water well and came to stand in front of the wooden shed, just as the moon peeked out from behind the dark cloud. The wood was worn, and moss grew up the sides, making it seem a part of the nature surrounding it.

Tom quietly stepped on the porch while she unlocked the door. His nearness made her ill at ease, and she dropped the key, but in one swift move, he caught it before it could drop to the ground with a clang. Then he unlocked the padlock and opened the door for Ursula to step inside. Now she really felt like *Dornröschen* in her castle.

"I'm afraid it's not much," Ursula apologized after lighting a kerosene lamp and carefully closing the door behind them. Despite the orders to evacuate the allotments after dark, one could never be sure there wasn't a soul to listen – and possibly report.

"It's about the same size as my cell, but at least I don't have to share it with two other men and stare out the window at the execution chamber anymore." He gave a sharp laugh, but Ursula didn't find it so funny, the skin around her blue eyes creasing as she frowned. She wasn't particularly religious, nor superstitious, but she did not think it sensible to blatantly tempt fate by mocking it.

"You can get water from the well and steal food from the soil at night. During the day, though, there'll be a constant rotation of people passing by. They won't be able to look inside, but nevertheless, you should stay inside the shed and make no noise." She gave him a stern glance and checked that the blinds were tightly shut.

The shed was filled with watering cans and various gardening supplies, including a rickety table and two sun loungers that had seen better times. She rummaged through the pile of neatly folded cloths in one corner and found the cushions for the sun loungers as well as a set of old but clean towels and several tablecloths.

"That will have to do for your bed." She knelt down to prepare his makeshift bed, but he grabbed her around her waist and gently forced her to stand up again.

"I can do that myself. You have done enough already." His green eyes turned into deep pools as he continued, "I owe you my life, Ursula Hermann, and know this, there's not a single thing I wouldn't do for you should ever the need arise."

His hands remained on her hips, burning a path through her clothes onto her skin and right into her heart. For a moment, she threw caution to the wind and pressed her body into Tom. After several days of nourishing food and normal rations, he'd gained weight, and even through his extensive layers of clothes, she noticed how his hard muscles now filled his big frame.

The urge to touch his rugged face became overwhelming, and she realized that her breath had quickened and her heart raced much too fast. She pushed her hands against his chest, frantic to get away.

"I have to go now. I'll come back tomorrow night with some food. Remember, don't leave the shed during the day."

Then she sprinted to the gate as if the devil incarnate were behind her. Only when she'd locked the gate from the outside did she close her eyes and breathe a heavy sigh.

CHAPTER 15

When Ursula went to work the next day, her mind lingered in the allotment with Tom. The way her body reacted to his nearness confused and worried her. She had loved Andreas, but he'd never caused those kinds of butterflies in her stomach.

Ursula put her troubling emotions aside and went through her routine, albeit without her usual cheerful smile. More than once, she overheard one of the prisoners asking what had happened to the Blonde Angel, although none of them dared to ask her directly. Not even her nickname drew a smile from her lips. Too strong was the anxiety about Tom's well-being, and the utter confusion about her feelings towards him.

It wasn't until the daily leisure hour that one of the older prisoners, not in age but in seniority, walked up to her when she stood alone and asked, "What's wrong, Frau Hermann? Shouldn't you be happy that the awful mass executions have finally ceased?"

Ursula nodded absentmindedly. "I should. And I am. I'm just...preoccupied."

The woman tilted her head and scrunched her nose. "Is this about your husband?"

In a prison like Plötzensee, news traveled fast, and most everyone knew about Andreas' death because she'd received one day of leave to visit the registry and run some other errands.

"Umm. Yes. I'm missing him terribly," she answered, happy about the excuse she could hang onto. It wasn't even a complete lie. She still missed Andreas, despite the current excitement in her life and the confusing feelings for the Englishman.

"I can sympathize," the woman said, and for a moment, Ursula thought she'd give her an embrace. But that was even more taboo than falling for the enemy.

"Thank you." Ursula dabbed at her eyes and quickly turned away, pretending to be needed somewhere else. Although this woman surely wouldn't utter a word to the authorities if she suspected Ursula was hiding an escaped prisoner, Ursula would have to maintain a better composure. If the prisoners noticed her anxious state of mind, her superiors might do the same. And Frau Schneider would ask harder questions.

Thankfully, the bell signaling the end of the leisure hour rang, and she was too busy to wallow in her thoughts.

The hours ticked by and Ursula longed to return home, though she knew the bubble of worry would not disappear there. But at least she wouldn't have to guard her agitation from others.

On her way to the staff room, she bumped into Pfarrer Bernau, jumping at the sight of him.

"Good afternoon, Frau Hermann, is everything all right?" he said in his sonorous voice.

She looked at him, frantic before her eyes darted up and down the hallway to make sure they wouldn't be heard. "I'm sorry, Father, but I can't do it. I just can't. I'm a bundle of nerves."

"Let's go to my room, shall we?" He turned around and then opened the door for her.

As soon as the priest had closed the door behind them, she blurted out, "I can't cope with the stress anymore. The entire day I was jumpy, afraid to give anything away. One of the prisoners even asked me what was wrong, and if Frau Schneider sees my agitation, she'll ask questions."

"Calm down, my child." Pfarrer Bernau put a calming hand over hers. "Nothing has happened."

"I'm just...I'm afraid someone will find out...things will go wrong. I have that terrible feeling." Ursula was on the verge of tears. She'd fought so hard to keep herself collected, her willpower was drained.

"Frau Hermann, you cannot give up now. This man needs you."

"But what if we are caught? What if I am killed? Or worse..." The dark visions loomed between them as they both had seen more evidence than any person should as to what happened with traitors. "I want to help, but I'm just some weak woman, not the material heroes are made of. Not like some of the brave women in here. It's only going to get harder and..." She was struggling to catch a breath, the intensity of her anxiety spilling out of her soaking up all her energy. "...I have reached my limit. I can't take it anymore."

"Please, just sit and breathe for a minute. It will all get easier."

Ursula didn't believe him for one second, but she forced herself to take several deep breaths.

"You must be scared. I know it, for I am scared too. But wouldn't it all be worth it, knowing you helped someone else?"

"I suppose. I just want it to be over. Living in constant fear isn't for me."

"It's only a few more days..." Someone knocked on the door, and Pfarrer Bernau called out, "One moment, please." Then he returned his dark eyes to Ursula and added, "I'm sorry, work calls. Can you come to the church this evening and we will chat some more? I might be able to give you a better indication of a timeframe by then."

"Thank you, Father, I'll drop by after taking care of dinner."

Ursula dragged her feet to the staff room and changed into civilian clothes. All she wanted was to curl up in her bed and spill her tears until she felt up to preparing food for Tom and making the trip to the allotments.

She got off the tram one station early and walked the rest of the way home. The September sun cast a golden glow on the leaves as it hung low on the horizon. The warmth of the day mixed with the chill the night would bring. She hoped Tom wouldn't be too cold in the shed at night. The exercise and the fresh air had calmed her down to the point that she hummed a melody in her head, confident over what the future would hold.

However, when she entered the apartment, her newfound confidence shattered to a million pieces as she found Anna standing in the living room, flanked by two men. All three of them turned around, and her heart sank into her stomach as she recognized the uniforms. Both men were in their early twenties, had broad shoulders, and wore their blond hair combed back with brilliantine. They looked dashing in their uniforms, and under different circumstances, she might have found their appearance pleasing.

"Ursula, these gentlemen are Gestapo. Frau Weber called them to report she heard noises coming from our apartment and thought someone was hiding in here," Anna explained, her voice calm.

Ursula froze in place, unable to move or breathe.

"Fräulein, we need to ask a few questions," the young, handsome officer said.

"Frau. It's Frau Hermann," Ursula corrected him out of habit.

"Frau Hermann," he answered with a frown. "Where is your husband?"

"Dead. He fell on the Eastern Front earlier this year." Her legs gave out, and if the second officer hadn't caught her, she would have fallen to the floor. He placed her onto the couch, his blue eyes looking at her with a mixture of suspicion and concern.

Then they started the inquisition. Ursula presented her papers and then answered endless questions about her whereabouts – if she'd noticed anything unusual, and so on. Much to her surprise, Frau Weber came out of the kitchen, holding up a dirty plate.

"He must have been eating from this plate," the neighbor said with the certainty of a woman who'd read too many mysteries.

"That's actually my lunch, but I hadn't had time to do the dishes before you arrived, gentlemen," Anna said with a well-calculated look.

"Someone was here. I heard the voice of a man. And footsteps," Frau Weber insisted.

Ursula didn't know what to say, but her sister was thankfully more quick-witted.

"Do you think someone broke in?" she asked the officer who'd smiled at her earlier.

"It might be a possibility," he hedged, trying to look stern.

"Oh, goodness. Imagine if my sister or I had been at home, who knows what this criminal might have done to us?" Anna's voice quivered, and expressions of shock and horror passed across her face.

Ursula could barely believe her eyes as she witnessed the spectacle.

A single tear ran down her sister's face, and Anna pressed a hand to her chest as she said in a high-pitched voice, "I'm so scared. The men of the family are fighting for our Führer at the front, and our mother is in the country. It's just the two of us."

Then she actually moved a step aside as if hiding from an unseen evil. "Do you think he's still here? What if he comes back? Who will protect my sister and me?"

Good grace, he has no idea he's being played. Anna was putting up an excellent show, her sobs as realistic as they could come, perhaps aided by the genuine severity of the sisters' current situation.

"We'll search the apartment to make sure nobody is hiding," the Gestapo officer smiled at Anna, and his eyes lingered a bit too long on her décolleté. Then he started opening every drawer and moving every piece of furniture around in his search for the hidden man. Anna followed him like a puppy, gasping little sighs of admiration for his strength and courage.

Ursula, though, didn't have to act frightened or worried – it was all natural. When she finally found the strength to get up from the sofa, she addressed the other officer. "Please, come with me. I'll show you the remaining rooms. I hope they didn't have time to steal anything."

While showing him Anna's room first, she racked her brain to remember if any traces of Tom's existence still remained in the apartment. She had cleaned and ventilated his room, changed the bedsheets, trashed his prisoner's uniform near Plötzensee.

An hour later, after no stone remained unturned, the two officers had to admit that there was no trace of an intruder to be found. Again, Ursula and Anna were questioned if anything was missing, or if they'd noticed a peculiar change, but the questions were much more benevolent, and Anna never missed a single opportunity to cast her big blue eyes at the Gestapo officer that had taken a liking to her.

Frau Weber insisted on her version of things, until the more serious officer had enough and exchanged a look with his colleague. Then he ordered her out of the apartment. She looked slightly shell-shocked but quickly pursed her lips and disappeared.

Ursula inwardly spoke a prayer that the harping vulture was gone.

Anna used the opportunity to up her game and looked up at the two young men with her big blue eyes while flicking her straight blonde hair back over her shoulder. Ursula noticed that her sister's neckline hung slightly lower than before and exposed just a hint of her breasts. The officer had noticed it too and kept his eyes glued to her skin.

"Thank you so much for making us feel safe again," Anna said with her best damsel-in-distress voice. "We are only weak little women, we have no hope of protecting ourselves against burglars – or worse." A shudder racked her frame before she focused on *her* officer. "You are a real-life hero. How can we ever thank you enough for your bravery and the service you do for our country? I would invite you for a cup of tea if that weren't inappropriate." She gave a slight eye flutter, and Ursula could not help being impressed.

"I'm afraid, Fräulein, we can't accept your generous invitation as it would indeed be inappropriate," the other officer said and cast a warning glance to his lovesick colleague.

Anna smiled gracefully and led them to the door.

Ursula heard the Gestapo cautioning her sister to always keep all the windows closed and the door tightly locked. When Anna sauntered back into the living room and flopped onto the sofa beside her, Ursula said, "That was magnificent, sister. Are you sure you want to become a biologist? Because I think your calling must be as an actress!"

Anna cuddled against her and giggled. "Told you it would come in handy one day."

"I'm just glad we moved Tom to the allotments last night," Ursula murmured and then leapt to her feet. "I completely forgot him. I have to bring him food, he must be so hungry."

"No. You can't leave now. We need to stay here. The Gestapo officers seemed to believe our story, but they might be secretly watching us now. Waiting for us to make a mistake and going to warn the man we were hiding. We can't risk that. Tom has to wait until tomorrow."

Ursula sighed. "You're right. I'll bet Frau Weber is pressing her ear against the wall, listening to our every step."

That night, Ursula and Anna slept in the same bed both as scared as if there truly had been a burglar in their apartment. They held each other closely as their minds raced.

"Are you asleep?" Ursula asked.

"No."

"What if we are caught? That was close. Too close. Imagine if Mutter hadn't decided to return to Berlin..." The unspoken threat hung in the air like a heavy burden pressing down on her chest.

"I'm scared too. But at least with *him* out of the house, we aren't compromised if he's caught."

Ursula inhaled deeply. She was sure Tom would rather die than betray them. And judging by his file, the Gestapo had already tried a vast number of different methods to make him talk. No, he wouldn't mention their names.

"What should we do now? I'm not sure I can keep this pretense up much longer. Today at work...one of the prisoners asked me if something was wrong. I'm not doing a good enough job hiding my emotions. What if someone else notices?"

"You started this thing, now you have to go through with it," Anna said. "I'm actually proud of you. My sister who's never broken the rules is smuggling a prisoner of war out of the country. How swell is that?"

A pink heat blossomed on Ursula's cheeks at the compliment. A pink that only intensified as the cogs in her mind turned, and something clicked into place.

"Oh no! I was supposed to visit with Pfarrer Bernau hours ago. He must be worried to death."

"Well, he'll have to wait, too. Visit him in the morning before you go to work. What would our new Gestapo friends say if they found us sneaking out in the middle of the night?"

"Goodness, I hope he doesn't come looking for me."

"He won't. No doubt, Pfarrer Bernau has lived through a situation like this more than once and knows how to behave." Anna pulled Ursula's head onto her chest in a warm embrace, the straight blonde hair mingling with blonde curls.

They lay there, holding each other all night. Ursula's stomach remained squeezed into knots, despite her sister's best efforts to set her at ease. Finally, she drifted off to sleep disturbed by troubling nightmares.

Ursula was running through an endless forest with something chasing her. But she could not see what it was, only sense its presence and that it was coming closer and closer and closer, no matter how fast she ran.

CHAPTER 16

W hen Ursula awoke the next morning, she sleepily stretched her arms and touched a human being lying in bed with her. She shot upright and gazed at her sister cuddling a pillow.

The events of the day before came rushing back. Ursula opened the blackout curtains, and sunshine streamed into the room. Reflections danced on Anna's nose and made her sneeze.

"Hey, sleepyhead, don't you have to work today?"

"Oh, for heaven's sake…" Anna leapt to her feet and stormed into the bathroom.

Ursula made breakfast for both of them, but Anna only grabbed a slice of bread with strawberry jam on the fly and rushed out of the apartment.

As soon as Ursula was alone, fear, guilt, and worry for Tom attacked her. She didn't dare to visit him in plain daylight, afraid people would start asking questions. He'd have to go hungry until the evening. She hoped he'd taken to picking the ripe produce from the garden last night.

She got dressed and loaded her handbag with a jar of jam,

crackers, a big chunk of cheese, canned beef, cooked potatoes, and curd. Then she left to visit Pfarrer Bernau in his parish before work. With a last glance in the mirror, she put a smart dark blue hat on her blonde waves. A thin half-veil covered her eyes and matched the pattern on her dark blue jacket. Then she wrapped a woolen shawl around her shoulders. The perfect outfit to visit church. Her newfound religiosity surely wasn't suspicious in these dire times.

"*Guten Morgen* Ursula, where are you headed?" Frau Weber pulled open her door the moment Ursula locked hers.

"*Guten Morgen*, Frau Weber. I'm going to church to offer a prayer of thanks that the burglar didn't cause us any harm." Ursula did her best to hide her scowl. Although she was rightfully annoyed, it was wiser to grin and bear it. Before the old witch could start a conversation, Ursula flew down the stairs and onto the street.

Crisp morning air whipped against her cheeks and she grabbed her shawl tighter. *Tom must've been so cold last night.* Those last summer days could still warm your bones, but the night temperature plummeted almost to freezing point.

She found Pfarrer Bernau near the altar, preparing his church for Mass that evening. A relieved smile crossed his face when he noticed the blonde woman coming up to him.

"Frau Hermann, it's good to see you." He looked around the church, empty except for an old lady kneeling with her rosary in the first row. "Are you here about the memorial service for your late husband?"

Ursula needed a few moments to grasp what he'd said, but then she nodded her head. "Yes, Father."

"Please come with me." He led her to the sacristy and closed the heavy door behind them. "I thought something awful had befallen you."

"It almost did." Ursula grabbed the back of a chair to still her trembling hands.

The priest turned to scrutinize her face. "You are scared, my child. What happened?"

"Do you remember my neighbor? She called the Gestapo on us."

The priests face paled, but he encouraged her to continue.

"Frau Weber insisted there was a man hiding in our place. They left nothing unturned and asked my sister and me thousands of questions."

"Did you tell them anything?" the priest asked with a deep frown on his forehead.

"No." Ursula shook her head, and her blonde waves bounced around her shoulders. "Actually, my sister flirted with one of the officers and made him believe that she was grateful that such a strong and virile man had taken to protecting her from the evils of this world. I was so scared..." She shuddered at the memory. "Without her..."

"You fared well because the Gestapo wouldn't have let you go if they'd had the slightest suspicion that you're not two innocent women."

"I know. And this is what scares me. My sister is so much better at this than I am. I have never learned to pretend, conceal, or deceive..." Ursula began pacing the room.

Pfarrer Bernau shrugged. "As your priest, I probably should advise you to stay honest and tell the authorities about the Englishman. But things aren't black and white. Right has become wrong, and wrong has become right. I myself have struggled with this notion for a long time, but in my prayers, God has led me to the conclusion that I have to answer only to my conscience and to Him."

Ursula tilted her head, surprised that a person as much at peace with himself and the world as Pfarrer Bernau possessed the same compunctions she had.

"After the Nazis came to power, I, like so many others, lived by their rules for many years. But one day more than five years ago I decided to stop obeying their unrighteous laws. Instead, I would follow my conscience, even if that meant being dishonest and conspiratorial.

"Since then, I have been organizing ways to hide Jews or help them escape our country. It is rewarding work, but you're right, it is very dangerous. And it is becoming harder by the day. People's fear of and allegiance to the Nazi regime is getting stronger, as is the regime's power to persecute and punish their opponents. Petty crimes are punished with an unprecedented cruelty to set an example and discourage others from opposing Hitler."

A shiver crawled up her spine and set her neck hair standing on end. He didn't need to go into details. Ursula's work was a constant reminder of what could become of her should she be caught. She had seen the varying states of people after being tortured, the psychological torment a death penalty placed upon people, and the general cruelty they endured in the prison.

Pfarrer Bernau closed the distance between them and placed his hands on her shoulders. His brown eyes fixated upon hers. "You have proven to be brave, and you possess a good heart. But you must know that you are risking your life in our line of work, as I have many times before. Many others who have helped have been arrested and killed. I don't say this to frighten you, but to alert you to be careful and never tell a single soul. Not even your mother when she returns home. The fewer the people who know, the safer it is for you – and for them. Do you understand?"

Ursula stared into his solemn face and nodded. Despite the gravity in his expression, she felt some small reassurance. She wasn't alone in this.

"Thank you, Father," she whispered and turned around to leave for work.

"Wait," he called after her, "if you visit Westlake, tell him that

I have a plan in mind and he might be back home within a week."

~

URSULA FINISHED her shift in the evening and entered a bakery. The enticing smell of freshly baked bread filled the air. She bought a loaf of dark bread that would keep fresh for a couple of days and couldn't resist a nut pastry for the walk. On second thought, she added another one for Tom as well.

As darkness settled, she arrived at the allotment and listened for footsteps before opening the gate, hoping nobody would hear the awful squeaking sound. But the gate swung silent as the night.

A smile brightened her face, and she carefully locked the gate behind her before walking up to the shabby shed. Her nerves tightened into a knot, and she had to set down the heavy handbag on the porch. No noise came from the inside, and she hesitated for a moment before opening the door. It swung open with unexpected ease, and as soon as she set a foot inside, she felt a gigantic weight pounce at her, like a lion after its prey. A big hand twisted her arm behind her back in a grip hard as steel, while the other hand covered her mouth, effectively preventing her from screaming.

Frozen with panic, she noticed out of the corner of her eyes when the door to the shed swung close. Complete darkness enveloped her. Her heartbeat throbbed against her ribs and indicated the seconds ticking by until she felt a warm breath against her neck and a familiar voice whispered into her ear, "I swear I'll kill you if you scream, understood?"

The tension left her body, and Ursula managed to nod in agreement.

"Why are you here?" the voice asked, and the hand slipped from her mouth to rest on her throat.

"It's me, Ursula. I'm here to bring you food," she said in a low voice.

His steely grip on her arm loosened, and he turned her around to press her front against his. Then he walked her a few steps like a puppet on strings until he found the lantern and flashed it into her face.

"Good lord, Ursula. I'm terribly sorry. I thought you were...well...here to arrest me," he said apologetically without letting her go. Instead, he squeezed her tighter and pressed his chin to the curve of her neck. "I was worried to death when you didn't return last night. The thought that something terrible had happened to you drove me out of my mind. You can't imagine how many times I was about to bolt and go after you."

"I'm fine," she answered, and he finally released her properly. She could still feel a tingle where his arms had been. It was so wrong to like the way he'd been holding her. Imprudent. Traitorous even.

Tom exchanged the lantern for the kerosene lamp and its soft light cast dancing shadows on the walls of the shed.

CHAPTER 17

U rsula watched how Tom hungrily wolfed down the food she'd brought.

"I'm sorry you had to go hungry, but it wasn't safe to come out here last night," she said.

Tom stopped eating for a moment and watched her closely, worry etched into his face. "What happened?"

"To make a long story short, our neighbor alerted the Gestapo that a man was hiding at our place." She noticed the way he gritted his jaw and his entire body tensed at the mention of the Gestapo.

"Are you all right?" He put down his food and moved to her side of the table, wrapping an arm around her shoulder. Warmth seeped into her body. With him by her side, she wasn't afraid.

"Yes. Thanks to Anna."

"Anna?"

"No need to worry. My sister put on a perfect show. She has that ability to make everyone believe she's holier than the Virgin Mary. It's something she has practiced since she was a toddler and always caught up in some kind of trouble. Anyhow, the

Gestapo believed her that we were just two weak women happy for them to protect us from any kind of evil." She scrunched her nose, and Tom had to laugh.

"Some kind of weak women you are...I've never met a stronger pair of sisters."

"Wait until you meet Lotte. She's a handful," Ursula slapped her hand over her mouth. The Englishman and her youngest sister would never meet. In a week's time, he'd be back in his country, and she'd never hear from him again.

Tom's voice grew soft. "I wish we had met under different circumstances."

"Me too," she said and gathered her things to leave. But leaving was harder than she'd thought. Too much did she enjoy being with him. "The gate doesn't squeak anymore."

"I thought I could make myself useful and oiled it." He cast her that boyish grin that always knocked her off-kilter. "And I fixed some loose planks in the shed, refilled the kerosene lamp, cleaned the sun loungers." He used his fingers to count the things he'd repaired.

"You didn't have to do that."

"I wanted to. And it kept me from barging out of the gate in search of you."

"I really should go." Ursula made an effort to stand up and grabbed her handbag.

"Yes, you should." His voice was throaty as he walked her to the door.

The moon was hiding behind a cloud, and not even stars lit the night. Before the war, Berlin had never been truly dark. The many lights always cast a dim glow into the night sky, but since the blackout rules had been put in place, it was as bleak as the countryside where her Aunt Lydia lived.

Ursula couldn't see her hand in front of her eyes and stumbled across a bump in the grass. She gasped in shock, but the next moment, Tom's strong arms were wrapped around her.

"Careful," he whispered into her ear. His face was mere inches from hers. She sensed it more than she saw it, although his fair skin glowed in the dark. Her brain was screaming at her to turn and run away. But she couldn't. A magnetic force drew her closer to him, and before she knew it, his lips touched hers in a soft kiss. For a moment, she savored the tingling excitement, gave in to the wave of emotions washing over her, consuming her. Then she pulled away.

"I...should go now," Ursula said as determinedly as she could muster.

"I'm sorry...I shouldn't have..." he answered in the same moment as the moon snuck out from behind the cloud and cast the landscape into its cold white light. Tom's face mirrored the same confusing emotions that whirled inside Ursula.

But before either one of them could utter another word, the night filled with the screeching sound of the air-raid sirens.

With the black humor of the truly desperate, Ursula told him, "Looks like your friends are visiting."

Tom stared at her as if she'd lost her mind until she pointed up into the sky. "Bomber squadrons."

"Oh...I'm sorry..." He shrugged his shoulders. There wasn't much he could say either way. This was war, and they stood on different sides. He knew as well as she did that they had only a few minutes until the first aircraft dropped their deadly freight somewhere over Ursula's city. "Please come with me inside."

Ursula felt a sudden sense of desperation. It was not safe for her to make her way home. Even if she reached any of the shelters, they wouldn't let her inside after the attack began.

"It's not that I have many choices," she sighed and followed him to the small shed.

"Stay here. I promise I won't kiss you again," Tom assured her.

She wasn't sure if she was relieved or disappointed.

They sat together on the sun loungers, talking, and even laughing as they got to know one another.

"Ursula, may I ask why you helped me, when you have never helped anyone else in this way before?" Tom's green eyes stared into hers. When she didn't respond, he ran a hand through his short hair and added, "I mean to say, what separated me from everyone else in my situation?"

Ursula tilted her head and thought for a moment. It was a question she had never really considered, but as she looked back, it was true that her attitudes toward the Nazis had changed significantly within the recent months.

"I think..." she said slowly, carefully considering each word. "That my perspective was changing. Like most everyone, I was supportive of Hitler at first. I thought he was doing good for our country. You know, bringing people back into employment, getting the economy back on track after the awful depression. But then I started seeing awful things. The prison, with all those women. And then, when Andreas died..." She fell silent.

"Who was Andreas?" Tom asked gently, taking her hand between his.

"My husband. He fell at the front a few months ago. It is his clothes you are wearing now," she admitted.

"I'm terribly sorry," Tom answered. The silence between them stretched to an awkward length before he asked, "Were you together for a long time?"

"Not really at all." Ursula gave a dry laugh. "We met nearly five years ago. We met at a flower shop, both of us buying flowers for Mother's Day. He had terrible taste, so I helped him choose them." A smile appeared on her face at the recollection of happier times – times without war. "He was handsome, dashing even." *Like you.* "And he was funny, always made me laugh. He charmed me straightaway and ended up walking me home. Before long, he asked me to go with him, and little by little we fell in love."

Ursula closed her eyes for a moment and then looked into Tom's face as if she'd just had an epiphany. "It was simple, you know? We were so happy and carefree. We never asked questions or doubted the fact that we'd grow old together..." her forehead wrinkled, "then he was drafted. He fought in France, Belgium, the Netherlands, and whenever he was on furlough, we made plans for after the war. Then he was sent to Russia, and things became dire. He convinced me to get married whilst he was away, just in case." Ursula's chest heaved with suppressed emotions threatening to burst out.

"He didn't come home for your wedding?" Tom asked, incredulous.

"No. It's quite common nowadays, and we call it *Stahlhelm-trauung* because I was literally saying yes to a steel helmet at my side." She gave a snorting cough. "You should have been there, it was eerie. Six women in the room and one steel helmet. The only man present was the registrar."

Tom squeezed her hand without saying a word.

"That was in January. Andreas never came home before he was killed in action," her voice had lowered to a whisper.

"I'm so sorry, Ursula. Life is not fair." He put his arm around her shoulders, pulling her against him.

She shouldn't allow him to do this, but the small gesture of kindness created so much comfort.

"You reminded me of him. In fact, when I saw you cowering in that crack in the wall, I thought about the women in your life and how they didn't deserve to suffer the same heartbreak I did. I'm sure a pretty girl is waiting for you back home?"

His face closed up as he shook his head. "No. She died during the Blitz."

"I'm sorry." For some odd reason, her heart sang in jubilation at the fact that he was a bachelor.

"Me too."

Ursula's eyes filled with tears of empathy and she snuggled

closer to him. Two grieving souls finding comfort in each other. Silence filled the shed, and they could hear detonations in the distance. *They must be bombing the other side of Berlin tonight.*

"Tell me about your life before the war. What's it like in England?" Ursula asked to distract herself from the bombers in the air and the attractive man at her side.

"I was a privileged idiot," Tom admitted with his signature grin. "It wasn't until the war that I even realized it. I went to boarding school and had grand holidays with my parents. Life for me consisted of fooling around and having fun. And flying…" His eyes took on a dreamy look. "My father is a pilot, and he started taking me with him as soon as I was able to walk. Those moments in the air are the most precious ones in my life. Up in the skies, the freedom is boundless. One day I'll show you–" His voice broke off when he realized what he'd said.

"Go on," Ursula said as if she hadn't heard the last sentence.

He told her about daily life in England. How much he missed his parents and his sister. The fellows on the base. Everything.

"The only real hardship I encountered was my awkward physical appearance as an adolescent," he smirked.

Ursula smirked back. "Please do tell." It was difficult to imagine the strong and handsome man as a lanky boy.

"Oh gosh, you really want to know the worst stabs to my ego?" he teased. When she nodded her head against his shoulder, he laughed and continued, "I was the last to grow among my friends, so I was at least a head and a half shorter than the rest. My voice was breaking, and I would squeak every other word." He imitated the sound and Ursula giggled uncontrollably.

"You're exaggerating," she insisted.

"Not at all. A pretty girl like you would have run as fast as your feet would take you. In fact, I remember the first girl I had a crush on. When I tried to kiss her once, she stumbled in shock

and fell backwards into the lake trying to dodge my advances."
His laughter was contagious.

"Oh, goodness!" She giggled and held her stomach. "Well,
you certainly don't have that problem anymore."

"I don't?" Tom asked raising one eyebrow. Ursula felt her
face turn a deep crimson under his piercing glance.

"No...well, I mean to say that you aren't odd anymore." The
more she talked, the worse she spluttered until she decided it
was better to keep silent.

"We should get some sleep," Tom said and stood to arrange
the two sun lounger pads side by side.

Ursula started feeling the cold mist settling in the shed the
moment she wasn't snuggled up against Tom's warm body. She
lay with chattering teeth on her pad, sparsely covered with one
of the tablecloths and her woolen shawl.

"Are you cold?" he whispered into the darkness.

"N...n...no."

"You're a bad liar, lady." He grinned and pulled her against
his chest. "Come here, I'll keep you warm."

Ursula wasn't sure what was worse – the awful cold without
him or the heat burning up her body as he held her in his arms.
She didn't dare move, and lay stiff until she heard his breathing
even out. Then she finally relaxed enough to close her eyes.

CHAPTER 18

The next morning, Ursula woke with the coming of dawn and snuck out of her makeshift bed. When she opened the door, sunlight fell inside. She took a few moments to observe Tom's peaceful sleep. She'd never seen him so relaxed. A half smile quirked up one corner of his mouth as he rolled to his side.

She quietly closed the door again, preferring not to say goodbye. The anxiety of the day before had been lifted from her shoulders, and she hurried home with lilting steps. Today was her day off from work, and while she would have liked to spend it in the allotment with Tom, prudence demanded she return home. She had plenty of chores to catch up with.

As she unlocked the door to her apartment, she hoped to find Anna still there. Anna probably was out of her mind with worry because Ursula hadn't returned home last night. But it wasn't Anna who was washing the dishes in the kitchen.

"Mutter. When did you get here?" Ursula asked, surprised. She had all but forgotten about her mother's plans to return.

"Late last night." Mutter dried her hands on her apron before she gave Ursula a curt nod. She held her daughter at arm's length, and a vertical wrinkle appeared on her forehead as she asked, "Where have you been? Anna said you were to come home before nightfall."

"I'm so sorry, Mutter, I was on my way home when the air-raid sirens shrilled. There wasn't enough time to get here, so I spent the night in a public shelter." Ursula lied without blinking an eye.

"Which one?" her mother asked and turned to continue with the dishes.

"About halfway from the prison," Ursula evaded. Rather than disappear into her room and cause more suspicions, she grabbed a towel and started to dry the clean dishes. "I'm glad you're back, Mutter. We missed you a lot."

A smile appeared on her mother's face. "I missed you too."

For a while, they worked quietly side by side, and Ursula allowed herself to relax.

"What happened to our food supply?" Mutter suddenly asked and turned to lock her eyes on her daughter.

Ursula felt herself shrink under the scrutiny. "What do you mean?"

"The pantry was stocked with cans, and at least half of them are gone."

"I'm sorry, Mutter. We ate some of them. We didn't mean to do anything wrong." Ursula resisted the urge to shuffle her feet or run away. Was this how her siblings had felt under Mutter's scolding stare throughout their childhood?

"Ursula Klausen, how can you be so imprudent? I always took you for the responsible one," Mutter chided her, using her maiden name. Ursula let the error slip, not wanting to add fuel to the fire. "Those supplies were reserved for emergencies. What shall we do if the food supply runs out? Or if your father and brother come home? What will we feed them on?"

Her mother yearned – like every German wife – for her husband to return from the front, even if only for a few days.

And the sorrow that clouded her eyes showed how much she feared for her only son, Richard, who'd been sent into hell at the tender age of seventeen.

Mutter had a good heart beneath her austerity, and she might have approved of feeding a sick and starving man. But not if that man was the enemy. Ursula couldn't tell her mother the truth. Not because she feared that Mutter would turn on her. But the words of the priest echoed in her head, that the fewer the people who knew, the safer it was – for her and for them.

"I'm so sorry, Mutter, it won't happen again. How is Lotte?" she asked, desperate for a change of subject.

"Your sister is fine, though she still dislikes the countryside. Goodness, she doesn't half complain about it either. My hopes are that she'll come to understand when she's older." Mutter suddenly looked drained, and Ursula remembered why her parents had sent Lotte away.

Her youngest sister was curious, outspoken, imprudent, impulsive, and always spoke before thinking. If she'd been here when the Gestapo searched the place, she would have given Frau Weber an earful. Ursula grimaced at the idea of how that would have worked out.

And she would certainly want to be involved. She'd jump up and down with excitement, ready to do something *useful* with her life. For Lotte's own good she was better off with Aunt Lydia in that godforsaken farming village, as far away from Berlin and the Nazi's full power as possible.

"Is she driving Aunt Lydia crazy too?" Ursula asked.

"No. I rather think Lydia has taken a liking to Lotte's antics. She finds her fiery personality a welcome entertainment, and your sister has been excellent help with my nieces and nephews."

"I haven't seen them in forever," Ursula mused.

"Oh, when you are allowed vacation, you must go and visit.

Kleindorf is such a pleasant and peaceful place. Lydia's children are absolutely charming, particularly the youngest. She looks a lot like you when you were that age." Mutter smiled at the prospect of better times after the end of the war.

"I will, Mutter," Ursula answered and hung the wet dishcloth on a hook.

It had been such a long time since she had considered anything beyond the present. When Andreas was still alive, she had fantasized about a family with three children, a house in the outskirts of Berlin and a life of tranquility. When he died, her future died with him.

Now, she wondered whether she might find happiness far away from home.

CHAPTER 19

U rsula and her mother spent the rest of the morning and early afternoon catching up on family news and on household chores. They gave the apartment a thorough cleaning and took stock of the inventory in the pantry. Somehow, Ursula managed to smuggle food from the kitchen into her handbag right under her mother's nose. Emboldened by her success, she tried again.

"What are you doing with the canned meat?" Mutter asked in a sharp voice.

Caught red-handed, Ursula's body tensed, and her brain frantically searched for a viable excuse. Lying to her mother wasn't something she enjoyed. But telling her the truth...even less.

"I thought we could celebrate your return and indulge with dinner tonight," she said with a firm voice.

"No." Mutter took the can from her hands and returned it to the pantry. "Haven't I told you that we need to be frugal? This is our emergency stock for bad times."

How much worse do times have to become to merit using our emergency stock? Ursula didn't dare ask aloud for she knew the answer. *A lot worse.* Her mother had lived through the hunger years after the Great War and the situation today was nothing compared to back then.

She'd have to find different ways to provide food for Tom, and hopefully not for long. *I should visit Pfarrer Bernau to find out how his plans are progressing.*

"Mutter, I'm going out," she called and put on coat and hat.

"Where to, darling?"

"Confession," Ursula answered as she slipped on long gloves and grabbed her heavy handbag.

"Since when did you become particularly interested in religion?" Mutter asked, raising an eyebrow in surprise. As a child, Ursula had been reluctant to go to confession.

"Only recently. I've found that it's helping me cope with everything going on at the moment," Ursula answered truthfully. Then she hurried to leave the apartment before her mother had a chance to deepen her inquisition. "I'll be back for dinner. Love you."

On the way to Pfarrer Bernau's parish, she was hung up in her thoughts. Despite the added complications Mutter's presence brought to her subversive actions it also took a heavy burden from her shoulders. It would be nice to return home after a grueling night shift and have breakfast ready. She could eat and fall into bed, instead of having to organize groceries first. But she and Anna had to maintain their secret under all circumstances. Mutter would never approve of the truth.

When Ursula found the chapel empty, she walked straight to the small house adjacent to the church that housed the priest's personal quarters. She raised her fist and knocked on the dark wooden door.

A visibly tired Pfarrer Bernau opened the door. His usually warm brown eyes were clouded with sorrow, and she could only imagine what awful things he'd had to witness today. At the sight of her, his face lit up.

"Frau Hermann, excellent timing. Please come inside."

"Thank you, Father, I'm here for confession," she said aloud just in case. Then she followed him inside and waited until he closed the door and offered her a seat in the office that also served as a visiting room.

"A few hours ago, this arrived." He waved an unfamiliar-looking identity card and handed it over to her.

"Teemu Miettunen, member of the Waffen-SS?" she asked as she studied the papers with Tom's picture on them.

"Yes. Because of Flying Officer Westlake's accent, we had to be a bit inventive. Teemu Miettunen is a Finnish soldier who joined the *Finnische Freiwilligen-Bataillon* two years ago, and upon disbandment of his unit three months ago, he chose to voluntarily continue to serve in the Waffen-SS. Unfortunately, he was severely wounded in combat and now has a medical permission slip to return 'home' to Finland together with a nurse."

Ursula couldn't quite follow all the details the priest and his helpers had made up for Tom's new identity.

"Don't worry. Here's a sheet of paper with all the details. Tell Westlake to learn everything by heart and burn the paper. Your task is to bring him to the Bahnhof Zoo tomorrow at nine in the morning and hand him over to our nurse. She'll take him to Rostock to board him onto a ship to Sweden."

"I can accompany him to Bahnhof Zoo tomorrow morning, but...he doesn't speak Finnish, and he's not blond either," Ursula insisted.

"You have been indoctrinated for much too long by the Nazi racial ethnology. While many Finns are blonde and blue eyed, there are also quite a few with dark hair. Just like there are Germans with dark hair. As for the language, that could be an issue," Pfarrer Bernau admitted before his mouth transformed into a big smile, "but I'm banking on the fact that nobody else in Germany speaks Finnish either. Police won't be able to distinguish an English accent from a Finnish one, and most likely won't even know this nation exists. It is the best solution we could come up with."

"I suppose it's better than keeping him in the allotment. My mother returned home, and smuggling provisions out of the house has become nearly impossible." Ursula curled a blonde strand around her finger.

"He will be fine as long as he sticks to the plan and speaks up only when asked." He put his hands on her shoulders and looked into her eyes, "Now, my child, are you ready to do this?"

No. "Yes," she answered with a trembling voice.

"Then hide these papers beneath your coat and go give our patient the good news."

Ursula nodded and left the priest's quarters. On her way to the allotment garden complex, the false papers burnt a hole into her skin where she'd stored the carefully folded sheets in her brassiere. The anxiety hurried her steps, and she reminded herself to keep an upright posture and a confident smile whenever she met a passer-by. She feared they were able to stare right through her layers of clothing and detect the hidden evidence. False papers. That alone was enough to sentence her to death.

Breathless, she arrived at the allotment just before dusk and found Tom tending to his injured thigh. The wound was healing well, and the black knots of Anna's stitches sat enthroned over pink skin.

A flush heated her cheeks at the sight of him in nothing but his underpants and a white cotton undershirt that showcased his broad shoulders and trim waist. Ursula quickly closed her eyes and only opened them at the sound of his chuckle.

"I'm not that ugly, am I?" Tom joked, amused by her embarrassment. He might have plenty of experience charming young women into his arms and bed, but Ursula wasn't used to seeing men in their underwear.

"No...I...can you get yourself modest again?" she stammered.

"By all means. My clothes should be dry by now. I washed them last night." He walked over to where he'd hung them over the window frame, and she couldn't help but notice the play of the muscles in his back. It was better for everyone if he left the next day.

They decided it would be best to meet where the path to the allotments branched off the main street. Then he would follow a few steps behind her until she handed him over to the woman posing as his nurse. The nurse would wear a Finnish flag pin on her lapel as an identifying feature.

The next morning, Ursula left her home with a pounding heart, perspiring cold sweat. Instead of walking the distance, she took the tram to work, got off after three stops and then took a bus, bringing her within a few hundred yards of their meeting place. She spotted Tom from far away as he walked out behind the hedges flanking the entrance to the allotments.

Without thinking, she raised her hand to wave at him, but caught herself and ran it through her hair instead. The plan was not to show that they knew each other. Pfarrer Bernau had insisted it was less risky. If he raised suspicions, she would still be able to walk away unscathed.

Despite the precautions, her anxiety intensified with every minute and the seemingly easy task to show him to the meeting point at Bahnhof Zoo grew into an insurmountable challenge. They reached their destination, and Ursula spotted the disguised nurse as she stepped away from the ticket counter, holding the train tickets in her hand.

Tom had caught up to Ursula in the multitude of people milling about, and she whispered, "See that woman over there? She must be the one."

"Yes, I can see a Finnish flag pin on her lapel. Goodbye and thanks for everything."

Ursula couldn't resist and squeezed his hand for a short moment before she let him go. In that same moment, the nurse spotted them and gave a barely visible nod. She still had a few steps to go until she reached the barrier where two uniformed men controlled papers and tickets.

"Papers and ticket please," a deep voice said.

"Here," the nurse answered with a smile and handed him her documents.

As he returned them to her, his eyes came to rest upon the badge on her lapel, and he broke out into a smile. "*Hyvää päivää.* It's rare to meet a Finn. My grandmother came from up there."

The nurse panicked and dropped everything on the spot, starting to run. But the policeman blew his whistle, and within seconds, the train station was infested with uniformed men.

Ursula watched with growing horror as they zeroed in on the nurse, then caught her, screaming and kicking. One of the officers took out his baton and soon blow after blow hit her, until she lay on the floor, her agonizing screams echoing through the air.

Ursula stood there, unable to move, oblivious to the danger to herself until she felt a strong tug on her hand. She tumbled against Tom, who put an arm around her waist and dragged her away from the scene. She put one foot in front of the other, grateful for Tom's steely grip that prevented her knees from giving out.

"Smile!" he commanded, and Ursula obeyed. She cast a weak effigy of usual bright smile at the crowd as they left the ugly scene just before the SS was done beating the nurse and started to close all doors of the train station in search of the person to whom the second train ticket belonged.

With every step away from the awful scene, Ursula's legs regained strength, and her smile became less forced. Tom released her waist, and they walked side by side in silence to the next bus station.

"I'll tell Pfarrer Bernau. He'll know what to do," she murmured. "I have to go to work now. Will you be able to find your way back to the allotment if I drop you off at the bus station nearby?"

"Certainly."

She believed him, but her mind still raced with worries. The fake nurse might give his cover name away, and they certainly could not return under this same ruse.

When she gave a heavy sigh, Tom turned to look at her. "Don't worry about me. I've been through worse."

She handed him the key to the allotment and whispered, "It's probably best if I don't return to the garden. My mother is suspicious enough, and the less time we spend together or sneak around, the safer it is for both of us."

"I agree." He looked straight ahead and they disembarked from the bus together.

"Remember that huge rhododendron marking the entrance to the allotments? I'll place a bag with food beneath it every day until we have another plan. You can sneak out at night to grab it."

"Thank you." He nodded and strode away as if they were strangers who had never met.

CHAPTER 20

U rsula impatiently did her work, looking for an opportunity to speak with the priest. As noon arrived, she finally spotted him during leisure hour. It was less than ideal, but she had to tell him.

Glancing at the prisoners and guards milling around, she approached him and said, "*Guten Tag*, Pfarrer Bernau, isn't it an awful day today?"

He didn't seem surprised, perhaps he'd already received the horrible news. "I know, Frau Hermann, I know. But we must have faith in God. You are invited to join the Mass in our church and go to confession."

Ursula nodded, not sure what he wanted her to do.

"So, I'll see you on Sunday in church for confession?" he clarified.

She nodded her understanding. "Yes, Father."

Sunday, that was three days from now. Hopefully by then, he'd have another plan to get Tom out of the country.

That evening, Ursula passed by the entrance to the allotments hiding part of the groceries she'd bought with her ration cards. Things had just become more complicated.

She decided to walk home and clear her head from the events of the day. The failure to get Tom on the train gnawed at her insides, as did the prospect of having to wait three days until she could visit the priest and find out what to do next.

Ursula had always prided herself on taking everything life threw at her in stride, to accept with humility and compliance what was expected of her. Her current anxiety was a new experience, one that scared her but also secretly thrilled her.

"Hello, Mutter, I already went shopping," she called from the door.

"Come in, darling," her mother answered.

Ursula stepped into the kitchen and almost dropped her shopping bag to the floor. Her mother was sitting at the kitchen table, drinking tea with Frau Weber. As far back as Ursula remembered, her mother disliked the nosy neighbor as much as her daughters did.

"*Guten Abend*, Frau Weber," she said tight-lipped and busied herself unpacking the provisions she'd bought.

"I was just telling your mother about when the burglar came," Frau Weber said, "and how odd it was that they left without taking anything, don't you think?"

Before Ursula could stammer a defense, her mother took matters into her own hands.

"We can only be grateful that nothing happened to my girls. The burglar must have been looking for something in particular and not found it, or realized he had been overheard," Mutter said firmly.

Frau Weber shook her head. "Hmm. I'm not so sure. There was something fishy about it."

"Frau Weber, I would appreciate you not accusing my children of improper behavior, particularly when you have no proof. Didn't you say that the Gestapo didn't find anything? I would guess it's more likely that you imagined the scuffle."

The neighbor looked like she'd bitten into a lemon and got

up without finishing her tea. "I better leave now, have a good night."

The second the door closed behind Frau Weber, Mutter turned to her daughter. "Now, Ursula. I know damned well that Frau Weber will not have imagined anything. She may be unbelievably nosy, but she is *not* losing touch. And I agree, it's quite clear there was no burglar here. Explain yourself."

Her mother's teacup was trembling in her hand, the china clinking against the saucer. Ursula shrank in size to a six-year-old being scolded. She couldn't tell her mother the truth, but she struggled to lie. She fumbled around looking for a plausible explanation, the pause stretching out.

"Ursula!" her mother insisted.

"I'm sorry. It was nothing, really. A friend needed a place to stay for a night. We just wanted to help." She pronounced the words carefully, intent on not flat-out lying, while not giving away her secret.

Mutter cast a glance that clearly indicated she didn't believe a single word, but at the sight of Ursula's thinly pressed lips, she sighed. "Believe me, I would send you away to the countryside this very moment if I could. Since when are you as irresponsible as Lotte?"

The door creaked, and Anna called out, "Hello, I'm home."

She came into the kitchen, and it took her only one look at their faces to know what was going on. She kissed both women on the cheeks and gave her sister a questioning look behind Mutter's back.

When they'd finished their dinner and washed the dishes, Mutter retreated into her room.

"What was that about?" Anna whispered, concerned.

"Let's go for a walk," Ursula suggested. They walked around the block, arms linked and eyes scanning for unwelcome listeners as Ursula recounted the events of the day starting with the scene at the train station and ending with Frau

Weber's accusations and the ensuing conversation with Mutter.

"Oh goodness, do you think she believed you?"

"Absolutely not, but she didn't persist. She must have sensed the truth wasn't something she wanted to know." Ursula tossed her blonde waves behind her shoulder.

"All's well that ends well." Anna fell into silence, but Ursula knew her sister too well. Something was bothering her.

"What is it?" she asked.

"Nothing."

They had reached the turn to their apartment building and would come to the entrance door within a minute if they turned right. Ursula tugged her sister's arm to the left. Anna sighed.

"Doesn't sound like nothing to me," Ursula sighed. Fear and anxiety held her in a fierce grip, but she'd rather die than not try to help her sister.

"Oh, God. Ursula, it's awful." Anna broke out in sobs. "I've been wondering about the unusually high number of deaths in the hospital. I mean, people are very sick, but the number of patients who died has skyrocketed in the last few months."

"It's not your fault, you know." Ursula knew that her sister suffered with each loss of a patient, sometimes blaming herself for not doing enough.

"I wish it was. Today, I overheard one of the doctors command the head nurse to make room in the hospital...by... how did he put it? 'Choosing those who had low hopes of recovering for a transport to another place.' When she objected that those patients weren't exactly transportable, he said it wouldn't matter. It would only save work if they died during the transport."

"No, that's not possible, Anna, you must have misunderstood." But deep inside, Ursula knew it was possible. Probable even.

"I'm telling you, it's the truth. They're murdering sick people in the hospitals. Not saving them." Anna's voice grew exasperated, and Ursula put a calming hand on her arm.

"Shush. Nobody would be that cruel." She longed for it to not be true, but as she thought about it, it surprised her less and less. Had she not seen the brutality of the Nazis this very morning? Beating down on a woman until she was unconscious? Torturing inmates at the Prinz-Albrecht-Strasse? It had always bothered her, but she'd justified it with the thought that those inmates were criminals. It had to be done to protect innocent citizens, to keep people like her safe from terror and attacks.

"Ursula, you don't understand. All the pieces fit now. There have been discrepancies, which I have questioned for months but not really given a lot of thought. *This* is the only thing that explains it all." Anna talked herself into a rage. "Leave your perfect world for one moment and think! Think of all the awful things happening, then explain to me how it can't be true."

Ursula knew there was no arguing with her sister. After the horrible mass executions at the prison and persistent rumors about murdering Undesirables, this was just another ugly piece to the puzzle of what the Nazis really were about. She'd lived in denial, closing her eyes and ears to everything that didn't fit into her rosy perception of the world. But all the time, the most awful crimes had existed right under her nose.

Torturing prisoners. Beating down women and children in open streets. Sending underage boys to the front. Persecuting entire segments of the populace and making them disappear. Ursula swallowed and put her free hand over her heart.

"What if you're right?" she said with a trembling voice.

"It's about time we stepped outside our protected bubble and saw the Nazis for what they really are: monsters more evil than the devil himself. I hate to say it, but Lotte was right all along. We have to stand up to what is going on in our country. Not just because we take pity on a cute fellow, or because we are in too deep now to get out, but because it's the right thing to do. Our allegiance shouldn't be with these monsters anymore – we need to listen to our conscience."

Ursula stared at Anna, torn between the urge to return to her former life and wanting to do what was morally right. She'd complained about the hardships of war and her awful job, but compared to how she'd felt the past weeks, it had been a piece of cake.

"It's not as simple as you're painting it. First of all, we don't have proof those killings are really happening..." She paused, tapping her lip with her finger. They didn't need proof. They'd seen enough other atrocities with their own eyes. "But even if it was, Germany is still our country. Hitler is still our rightfully elected Führer. How can we align ourselves outside of our Fatherland? Betray it?"

"Just think of those people who are being killed every day. Hitler has just announced Berlin is free of all Jews, but where do you think they are? Are they in prison?"

"No...they have been relocated. Somewhere. In Poland. To start a new life away from Germany, where they can't ruin our country."

Anna snorted. "You still believe this shit? After all that you've seen for yourself? After the troubling news the priest told you?"

Ursula bristled, defending her view of the world. "He hasn't been there. It's only hearsay." Anna couldn't just tear down her entire belief system with a few words. That would leave her naked, unprotected, floundering without anything to hold on. How should she live without rules in place that told her what to do – and what not to do? What would happen to her beloved country if everyone did as they pleased and disregarded the laws? Wasn't that the first step into absolute chaos? Doom for everyone and not just for a few?

"Take off your blinders and see things for what they really are!" Anna's voice was high-pitched with agitation. "What do you think happens to people who are relocated? They are being slaughtered in concentration camps, Ursula."

"Shush, someone might hear," Ursula warned her sister. At the same time, she felt dirty. Ashamed that she had never known what was happening nor *tried* to find out. Like a good obedient citizen, daughter, and woman, she'd ignored the brutality and believed the propaganda fed to her day in day out.

"See what I mean? We can't even speak out anymore. We're afraid to be thrown into prison for the crime of voicing our discontent. *This* is not our Germany anymore. This is a regime of injustice, and I, for my part, don't want to be a part of it anymore. Do you?" Anna glared intensely at her.

No, Ursula thought, but she was too afraid to speak aloud.

CHAPTER 21

The wireless brought news the next day of plans to evacuate all civilians not directly aiding the war effort in Hamburg to Rügen. The second largest city in Germany had some time earlier been the target of an awful attack by the English and American bomber squadrons.

It was known under the name of Operation Gomorrha, and as far as Ursula – or anyone else for that matter – remembered, it was the most horrible and devastating attack ever flown against her country. Apart from killing more than forty thousand civilians and wounding thirty-seven thousand, the firestorm it created had destroyed most of the city.

One of her former inmates – Hilde Quedlin, may she rest in peace – had received a letter from her relatives in Hamburg with a graphic description of the horrible scenes. Because the summer had been unusually hot and dry, the bombs created an effect never seen before. Ursula hadn't exactly understood the details, but apparently, the dry buildings and trees had caught fire immediately, causing a vortex of hot air that created a cyclonic fire rampaging across the city and leaving a trail of complete destruction in its path. The asphalt on the streets burst into flames, as did the oil-saturated water of the many canals and the harbor. Eyewitnesses told about people being sucked into the fire like feathers right in front of them as they hurried to get to safety.

Most of the fatalities didn't occur due to burning, though, but in the treacherous safety of the underground bomb shelters. The fire raging above consumed all oxygen and the people suffocated. Ursula shivered at the thought of asphyxiation and involuntarily cleared her throat.

When she finished her household chores, she put on her best dress, the one she'd worn for her wedding, together with a hat and gloves.

"Mutter, Anna, I'm going to church," she called out and stepped out the door. After mother's scolding, Frau Weber didn't dare to openly harass them anymore, but Ursula heard the telltale click of the peephole in her door.

After Mass, Pfarrer Bernau spoke to many of his parishioners, giving each of them a few words of encouragement, while Ursula impatiently waited her turn.

"Frau Hermann, it's good to see you. Will you join me in my office in ten minutes to finalize the details for your late husband's memorial service?"

"Of course, Father, thank you for your kindness," she said and turned to wait at the door to the sacristy, which had a connection to his private quarters.

Ten minutes later, the church had emptied, and he arrived to lead her to his office. After carefully closing the door, he motioned for her to sit down.

"Do you have news for me?" she burst out.

Pfarrer Bernau chuckled. "Good things take time to ripen. But yes, I have a plan. It's a long shot, but probably our only chance. That is...if you agree."

"Me? Of course," Ursula answered, her feet tip-tapping on the parquet flooring.

"Hear me out first and then decide."

His authoritative tone made goosebumps rise on her arms. "Fine."

"Sometimes God sends us an opportunity disguised. We simply have to listen and understand. After hearing about the evacuation of residents of Hamburg to Hitler's unfinished luxury hotel in Prora on the island of Rügen, I had an idea. Flying Officer Westlake can pretend to be a resident of Hamburg who has been bombed out."

"But his accent...they'll never believe he's a German," Ursula protested.

The priest smirked. "That's why he's mute and mostly deaf. Shell-shock. He's been discharged from the Eastern Front because of severe injuries. If you manage to get sent with the other civilians to Prora, then there's a merchant ship waiting for him three days from now in Sassnitz to get him to Trelleborg in Sweden."

"But without papers, how can we prove any of this?" Ursula asked, confused. The tip-tapping of her toes stopped for a moment as she tried to wrap her brain around the words of the priest. It didn't make sense.

"This is where you come into play. I have to warn you, though, it's extremely risky, but may be the only way to make it work." Pfarrer Bernau leaned back in his chair and folded his hands across his stomach as if in prayer. "If you travel with him as his *wife*, letting him use the papers of your late husband, it might work. I can have the photo switched out in time."

All the blood drained from her face, and she studied her toes.

"Don't jump the gun on this decision. It is grave. If you are caught, nothing will save you. Not him. And not you," the priest enjoined her.

"I will do it," she whispered.

Ursula left the priest determined to set the plan in action

141

before she lost her nerve and changed her mind. She took the bus to the allotment gardens and ran straight to the small patch her family owned, foregoing the agreement to deposit a note. This was too urgent.

"Tom! Open the door, it's me, Ursula," she whispered urgently as she tapped on the door of the shed. Tom opened it looking as though he had just woken up. Since he couldn't go out during the day, he spent his days sleeping and his nights doing whatever he needed to do.

Ursula pushed straight through, not wanting anyone to notice her presence.

"Bloody hell, Ursula, you gave me a fright. I thought we agreed you wouldn't come back here," Tom said and yawned.

"I know, but I couldn't wait. The day after tomorrow, we'll try again." She breathed hard, barely getting the words out.

"Come on. Sit down and relax. Do you want some water?" He moved to the cupboard where he'd stored water in a carafe.

Ursula sat down and caught her breath. Then she detailed the new plan. Tom listened intently, shaking his head to the right and the left. When she ended, he looked at her for a long time.

"No. It's too dangerous," he said with arms crossed in front of his chest and his feet planted on the ground at hips' width.

"But it's a unique chance. There's a merchant ship sailing three days from now. It will take you to safety." Ursula pleaded with him.

"No. I won't allow you to risk your life for me."

"What have I been doing up till now then?" she asked. "In fact, I will only be safe again when you're gone. The Gestapo isn't stupid, and as long as you're in Germany, you're a threat to my safety."

He stared at her for a long time and then said, "All right. What's next?"

"I'll tell you some more about Andreas. After all, you'll be him." She smiled sheepishly, wishing for a moment he could really become her husband and not only pretend.

They sat down together, and she instructed him about everything there was to know, reminding him that from the time he left the allotment until he reached the ship he was supposed to be mute, deaf, and limping.

"We'll meet the day after tomorrow at seven a.m. at the bus stop. Don't be late," she said as she prepared to leave.

"How could I leave such a beautiful woman waiting?" he teased, and the blood shot to her face. If she'd had the time to think through the plan properly, she would have refused. Now, it was too late.

That night she told Anna about the plan. Her sister seemed torn between admiring Ursula's courage and questioning her mental health.

"God help us, sister. I won't have a moment's peace until you return." Anna wrapped her arms around her sister. They clung to each other like castaways to a safety buoy.

"Anna. I will be gone for two days. What shall we tell Mutter?" Ursula whispered.

"Be glad that you have me," her sister teased. "In the hospital, they were seeking volunteers to accompany the evacuees in their off time. We'll tell her you're doing just that. And it's not even a lie…"

The next morning, they told Mutter about Ursula's volunteer work.

"I don't understand why you have to do this." Mutter shook her head. "Where will you sleep?"

"Mutter, I'm sure we'll be taken care of," Ursula answered.

"Maybe I should phone the officer in charge to recommend you," her mother replied with anxiety and dried her hands on her apron as if she intended to use the phone right now.

Ursula's legs were close to giving out, and she might have fainted if her sister hadn't intervened.

"Mutter, please. Ursula is an adult. How will she look if her mother calls to make sure she's safe?"

"I don't know..."

"We were fine while you were gone; it really is no big thing." Ursula tried to set her mother's mind at ease.

"About that...knowing how much you two dislike gardening work, I plan to visit the allotment today."

"You can't..." Ursula blurted out before she caught her lapse and continued in a much calmer voice. "You just got here, and you must be tired."

"I arrived more than a week ago." Mutter pressed her lips into a thin line.

"Ursula and I have been taking care of everything. There's nothing that needs to be done." Anna came to her sister's help, but to no avail. If anything, she'd managed to raise their mother's suspicions.

Mutter put both fists on her hips and stared at her daughters. "What exactly are you hiding from me?"

Ursula squirmed under the scrutiny. As much as she wanted to, a direct lie to her mother would never leave her lips.

"I can't say. And for your own sake, you'd rather not know. Please, can you wait just one more day? I promise it'll all be over by then." Ursula wrung her hands, willing her mother to agree.

Her mother sighed, pressing her palm to her temple. "You are right. Taking my cue from Frau Weber and your strange behavior, I'd rather not know. I can only pray to God that whatever you're doing isn't rash and immoral. I should never have left you without my supervision, but who could divine that the two of you would take after Lotte?" With these words, Mutter turned around and disappeared into her bedroom, leaving two completely perplexed daughters behind.

"Did she really say this?" Anna murmured. "I feared she'd ground us without food until we told her the truth."

"I'm sure she already figured a version that's very close to the truth and decided she didn't want to know…" Ursula's heart was still beating in staccato. She dried her sweaty palms with a dishtowel and added, "I'll have to go to work. See you tonight. Love you, sister."

At work, she arranged for a colleague to cover her shifts for the next two days in exchange for her working the next two weekend shifts. When she returned home in the evening, her mother had already retreated into her room, which Ursula was actually thankful for. It would only be awkward to sit together and *not* talk about the one topic that was on everyone's mind.

The next morning, she gathered Andreas' papers that had been sent to her after his demise, hugged her mother and her sister goodbye, and walked to the meeting place with Tom. Her wedding band glittered golden in the sun. *It's actually a good thing I'm still wearing it.*

He already waited for her, meticulously dressed and combed. She gave him his papers, and he took her arm like any gallant husband would. A tingle crept down her spine.

"Are you ready to do this?" He smiled at her.

"No, and I don't think I ever will, but let's do it anyways." Ursula gave a nervous laugh and was thankful for the confidence he exuded.

"That's the way I like my girls. Valiant and never losing their humor." He pecked her cheek and the tingle in her body intensified.

"I'm just glad you won't be able to talk for the rest of our journey," she retorted and reveled a tiny bit in the sight of his dismayed face.

Then he raised his hand to his lips and made the gesture of turning a key and throwing it away. A few minutes later, they boarded the bus that would take them on the same journey to Bahnhof Zoo they had taken only a few days before.

She bought the tickets without any problems, papers were checked and checked again, and nobody raised as much as an eyebrow. When they finally found a place on the train, she slumped against the backrest with a sigh loud enough to make the other passengers look.

Ursula glanced into tired, worried faces. Faces that told of awful experiences, of horrible fear, and of the hope to escape their nightmares. She wondered whether all of them were evacuees. Despite the masses of people, there was very little chatter, and the atmosphere remained cold.

As much as she yearned to talk to Tom, they had to maintain the ruse at all cost. It was his only chance to leave Germany alive. So, they sat in silence holding hands throughout the entire journey.

Several hours later, the train stopped in Stralsund.

"Endstation."

Tom sent her a questioning glance.

"The conductor said this is the terminal station, but he didn't say why. It looks like we have to walk the rest of the way." She spoke with exaggerated movements, as if she wanted him to lip-read her words.

They disembarked from the train together with several hundred other passengers. All of them headed toward the island of Rügen that connected to the mainland via the Rügendamm, a two-and-a-half-mile-long bridge. Word traveled that the train had to return and evacuees were supposed to walk across the bridge.

Ursula and Tom followed the long line of people ahead. It was a sad procession of people crossing the immense bridge. Determination dominated their faces, and no one stopped to talk to others as they would have done before the war.

Most of them carried suitcases or other luggage. Ursula assumed it was everything they had left in their possession after being bombed out. Like most people, her mother had deposited suitcases with friends and family in houses at different corners of Berlin in case they lost their home. Then they would at least have the bare necessities. Two of their four suitcases had already gone up in flames together with the belongings of the family residing in that house.

She and Tom were asked for their identification papers upon disembarking the train, and again just before setting a step on the bridge, but in the hustle and bustle, it seemed no one noticed that they did not fit in with the rest.

Ursula was too occupied with her own thoughts to give much attention to the beautiful landscape surrounding her. The view down from the bridge across the Baltic Sea sparkling in the sunshine would have been spectacular. A soft breeze blew the smells of salt and fish into her nose, combined with the taste of fresh earth and grass. She pushed a strand of hair from her eyes behind her ear.

The afternoon sun shone bright and would have dazzled her if she hadn't kept her eyes looking at the ground. With every step she took, her inner turmoil increased. Yes, she wanted to get Tom to safety, but she also dreaded the time to say goodbye. As soon as she delivered him to his contact person on the ship, she'd make her way back. He'd leave without having left a trace, and soon, he wouldn't be more than a ghost lingering in her memory.

CHAPTER 22

The Island of Rügen loomed on the horizon, and it wasn't more than a hundred yards before the bridge ended, and they would step onto the island. But the trek slowed down. SS and border police demanded to see papers again.

"Papers, please," an SS officer said.

Ursula handed over her and Tom's papers, while Tom stared at the ground, his mouth half open while incessantly nodding his head.

"These papers are not valid."

Ursula almost toppled over at the impact of his words. If it weren't for Tom's unforgiving grip on her hand, she would have dumped everything and started to run – like the fake nurse at the train station. And she'd probably end up the same way...

"Why, sir? Our papers..." Ursula's breath came in ragged spurts.

The SS officer turned to Tom, completely ignoring Ursula. "You and your wife are currently registered in Berlin. The buildings at Prora are specifically designated for evacuees from Hamburg. Didn't you know this?"

Tom raised his head when the officer took a step closer, and kept nodding with something similar to a smile.

"Officer, my husband can't hear you," Ursula addressed the police officer. "He came home from the front mute and deaf. Shell-shocked, the doctor said."

The SS officer looked uncertain. Tom edged closer to her as if he were afraid, drool dripping from his lower lip.

"I thought we would be better off out here because the constant air raids in Berlin make him worse. The doctor said my Andreas might regain some of his senses if I can take him far away from the impacts of war." Ursula was proud of herself. Apparently, Anna wasn't the only one with acting abilities in the family.

"I honor the sacrifice your husband made for our country, Frau..." he checked the papers that he was still holding in his hand, "...Hermann. But orders are orders. I can't permit you to enter Rügen. You must return to the mainland." He handed the papers back to her.

Ursula wanted to jump with joy because he hadn't arrested them, but instead, she said with a solemn face, "Thank you, Officer." A huge sigh escaped her lungs as she turned to her *husband* and tugged his arm to make him aware they had to turn around.

"*Gnädige Frau*," the SS officer called after her when she'd gone less than three steps. The blood froze in her veins, but she turned around.

"Yes, Officer?"

"In Stralsund, take a bus to a village called Jakobsdorf. If you are willing to work hard, tell the mayor you came recommended by *SS-Sturmmann* Kunze."

A smile crossed her face. "Thank you for your kindness, Officer Kunze."

The trek back across the bridge was even more depressing. Now they faced the tired, despairing, and pained faces of the evacuees and had to push against the stream of people. Instead of looking onto the green island of Rügen lying like a jewel in the Baltic Sea, they now faced the ancient Hanseatic City of Stralsund with its signature red-brick buildings.

Under normal circumstances, Ursula would have appreciated the beauty of this city, but now it only reminded her of their failure – again. Tom was returning to the German mainland, every step taking him further away from freedom.

Once they had reached their starting point again, they wandered away from the crowd until they found a secluded place on the beach, where they fell into the sand, leaning against each other.

"Oh God, Tom. What are we going to do?" Ursula asked with desperation.

"Don't worry. We're still alive. We'll find another way to get on the island." He wrapped his arms around her, spreading comfort. "You should return before it gets too late."

Ursula leaned her head against his shoulder. "No. Without me, it will be even harder for you to find your way to the Swedish ship. Who knows how many more checkpoints are on Rügen."

"Ursula…"

She pushed against his chest and glared at him, "I haven't come so far to leave you here to your fate. I will stay with you until I've handed you over. And I won't discuss this any further, understood?"

"Your glare is deadlier than a stab with a bayonet, Frau Hermann," he chuckled.

"Ugghh…you…you…" She couldn't think of an appropriate word to use, and the puppy look in his eyes didn't help to keep her focus on being angry with him. "The ship sails tomorrow in the afternoon, but we need to be in Sassnitz in the morning to meet the contact person with your new papers. You'll be a Swedish merchant in the ore business."

"That's quite a step up from being deaf and dumb." He grinned. "Although I was beginning to enjoy having you at my beck and call."

Ursula swatted his arm. "This is not the time for jokes, Flying Officer Westlake."

"Oh? Then when's the time for jokes? When I'm buried six feet deep?"

A shiver racked her body. Danger followed them with each step they took, and the possibility of dying before he reached the safe ship wasn't very far away.

"You worry too much, my dear." Tom wrapped his arms around Ursula, pulling her close into his chest. He rested his head on hers, the blonde waves soft against his face. "There will be another way, I promise."

CHAPTER 23

Once Tom had comforted Ursula and convinced her that there was still a hint of hope, they began discussing alternative methods of reaching the island. The only way by foot was along the bridge, which was far too risky now.

"We will need to cross the water somehow..." Tom leaned back on his elbows and looked across the Strelasund, the sound between the mainland and Rügen. The evening sun was hanging low on the horizon, casting a golden glow across the water. The island of Rügen rose from the sea, so near and yet so far. He sighed deeply.

Ursula got the idea that he was yearning for a much bigger island as he looked westward into the sun.

"It's too far to swim, we'd drown. Besides, if we arrived on the other side sopping wet, it would raise suspicion." Ursula murmured. She knew how to swim of course, but she'd never done it for more than a hundred yards at one of the popular bathing beaches in Berlin.

"Agreed, we need to blend in with the evacuees. We need a boat." He leapt to his feet and pulled her with him. "Come on, let's see if someone will give us a ride."

They walked along the water's edge, looking for a boat. The sun soon disappeared behind the horizon, and within moments, the warm September evening gave way to the chilly night. A few minutes later they came upon a small fishing harbor, where countless boats were tied to a rickety wooden walkway over the water's surface.

Tom assumed his role as a Swedish merchant needing to find a way across the Strelasund, and walked up to countless fishermen, asking if he could rent their boats for the night. But all of them said no – a concerned and suspicious look on each one's weathered faces. Finally, just as Ursula was giving up hope, the owner of an old and shabby rowing boat agreed to lease it to them. He greedily took the money they offered and warned them not to use the outboard motor, as that would alert the border post.

The fisherman didn't ask any questions, and Ursula got the impression that he was as keen to keep away from the authorities as they were.

"Wartet auf die Nacht und immer schön links halten, sonst werdet Ihr ans Festland getrieben," the fisherman mumbled.

Tom cast her a questioning look, but Ursula shook her head. Only when the fisherman had disappeared did she repeat his words. "He told us to wait for nightfall and row toward the left, or we'll drift back to the mainland."

"Good to know." Tom grinned. "I didn't understand a single word, what language was he speaking?"

"Some mumbled dialect. I, too, had difficulties understanding."

They sat on the pier, a bollard shielding them from unwelcome eyes and ate their provisions as they waited for the darkness to settle.

"Do you think we will make it?" Ursula whispered.

"I do. I think things are just beginning, you know?"

"I really hope they are. I hope everything will change. You

will return home, and the war will end and then..." She bit her lip, not wanting to give away her thoughts.

"Then what?" Tom asked, his emerald green eyes holding her captive.

"I don't know...maybe then we could see each other again," she admitted, feeling heat rise to her cheeks.

"I would like that a great deal." He took her hand and squeezed it for a moment. "Come along, it won't get any darker than this and we have a long way to row."

The boat creaked and swayed as he helped her climb in. It was pitch black by now, the only light the reflections of the stars on the crevices in the ocean's surface. The Strelasund was protected from wind and waves by the island, which made their traveling relatively easy. But the farther they veered away from land, the more the temperature dropped, and Ursula wrapped her shawl tighter around her shoulders.

She sat looking forward and gave Tom directions to steer toward the dark silhouette of the languet the fisherman had indicated as the most inconspicuous landing area. By the time they'd reached the halfway mark, she was being whipped by salty spray and crisp winds. Their only conversation was hushed whispers of "left" and "right" that nonetheless echoed across the water, sounding like yells in her ears.

"Stop," she whispered as a grumbling sound reached her ears. Tom froze in place, the oars sliding gracefully through the water with nothing more than a gurgle. In the distance, they heard pounding, shouting, then it was silent again.

They waited motionless for another minute until Tom took up the rowing again. Ursula shivered in the chilly night air and prayed she would leave this boat alive. Drowning would be an even worse death than asphyxiation. Involuntarily, she grabbed the rail tighter.

After what seemed like hours, they reached the shore. Not a soul was to be seen and judging by the disarray of flotsam on the beach, this part of the island wasn't visited frequently. The fisherman had given them excellent advice. They hadn't asked how he would recover the boat, but Ursula was sure he had his means.

Tom dug the oars into the sand to push them forward silently, not daring to make a sound even through the gentle splashes of water. Once close enough to the dry sand, Tom and Ursula leapt out of the boat. Then they hid the boat near a rock and climbed the dune in the direction of northeast. She marveled at Tom's uncanny ability to discover the cardinal direction simply by looking at the sky.

Soon, they reached a street. Several minutes later, a sign indicated they were on their way to Sassnitz. Luckily, a truck with evacuees stopped and the driver told them to hop on. It was way past midnight when they finally arrived at a house where their contact person handed them Tom's Swedish papers and a ticket for the ship from Sassnitz to Trelleborg.

The widow, who had rented out rooms in her beachfront property before the war, now catered to the few merchants coming from Sweden or Denmark. She'd known Pfarrer Bernau from thirty years back before she had married into Rügen. Now she helped him once in a while hosting guests that otherwise wouldn't be rented a room.

She showed them the room and Ursula glared in shock at the big matrimonial bed. She wasn't expected to share her bed with a man, or was she? As strange as it sounded, that thought, which frightened her almost more than having to brave another SS officer, also sent an unusual heat into her body.

"I'll get ready for bed," she whispered and escaped into the bathroom, carefully locking the door behind her. She took her sweet time changing into the cotton nightgown that reached to her ankles, combing her hair until it shone, brushing her teeth, and everything else she could think of, hoping Tom would fall asleep meanwhile.

"Oh, I say. You look peachy," he complimented her and stood. He took her hand and raised it to his lips, pressing a soft kiss on the back of it. "Thank you for everything you've done for me."

Ursula cast her glance away. It was strange. They had known each other for such a short time, yet she felt as though Tom was a part of her.

Tom took her chin into one hand and softly turned her head, so she had to look into his green eyes. Then he asked with a soft voice, "Will you be all right, getting back to Berlin on your own?"

"Of course I'll be fine," Ursula answered. But a sudden weight pressed on her chest and made breathing difficult. How could she ever be fine with the certainty that she'd never see him again?

"Good." The silence lingered again, intensified by their inability to look away from one another.

"I'm going to miss you, Tom," she whispered.

"This doesn't have to be the end forever, Ursula. If you don't want it to be," he murmured, his eyes never leaving hers. She'd never gazed into such deep pools. His eyes betrayed his true feelings for her, but she also saw her own confusion and worry mirrored in them. He was still the enemy.

"Do you want it to be?" Her words were barely audible. She was afraid of the answer. Afraid he would say yes. But equally afraid he'd say no. There was no conclusion to their dilemma, and there would never be a happy ending.

"Not for a second." Tom's eyes shone with honesty as he ran a hand through his cropped dark hair. "I have never met anyone as brave or caring as you, Ursula. I owe you my life, but that's not the only thing. You have captured my heart and my soul. My entire being belongs to you and will continue to do so forever. I don't care whether our countries are at war, and we're supposed to be enemies. I love you."

Ursula's jaw dropped open, and she blinked. At a loss for words, she stood motionless when his hand reached out to stroke her hair. She didn't move when his fingers caressed her cheek. And she didn't resist when he pressed a soft kiss on her lips. But when he swooped her up into his arms and carried her over to the bed, she threw her arms around his neck, her body trembling in anticipation of what was to come.

CHAPTER 24

The next morning was crisp, and a gentle mist hung in the air softening the pale blue light. Ursula and Tom awoke tangled in the white bedsheets, holding onto each other like castaways in the ocean. They got up and dressed in silence. Now that the end of their time together approached, no words were the right ones.

They walked the three miles to the harbor of Sassnitz. From far away, they discerned the Swedish flag fluttering in the wind high up on one of the ships.

Ursula's nerves were tied into knots. They were so near to success, yet so much could still go wrong. Tom walked by her side with the confident stride of a wealthy merchant untouched by the war raging across Europe.

A small smile tugged at her lips at how well he'd lived up to the different roles he'd been forced to play. But maybe when you were on the brink of execution, everything that promised hope was an easy task.

The island of Rügen was especially beautiful that morning. The grass glistened with dew, and a deep blue strip of the ocean was painted along the horizon. Several times, they stopped to catch a glimpse of the majestic white chalk cliffs.

"They resemble the White Cliffs of Dover," Tom said, and his eyes took on a yearning glow.

"You're homesick, aren't you?" she asked him, interlinking her fingers with his.

"I am, but..." He didn't finish his sentence and looked away. There wasn't much to say. Some things simply couldn't be changed.

As they approached the port, she asked, "Are you sure the border post won't distinguish your English accent from a Swedish one?"

"As long as they don't speak Swedish, I'll be fine," he chuckled.

Ursula stopped and cast him a fearful look, remembering their fake Finland nurse. "Oh goodness, I hadn't thought about this possibility. What if..." A kiss sealed her lips and prevented her from finishing her sentence.

"You worry too much, my darling. Now that I can see the ship and taste freedom, I won't let those bloody Jerries catch me again..." One look at her face silenced him, and his ears turned crimson red. "I'm sorry. I...I didn't mean you, of course."

"I know." Ursula put a hand on his arm. "This is one more reason for you to leave."

Once at the port, they embraced one another tightly, unwilling to let go. Tears streamed down Ursula's face, and she could see them sparkle in his eyes too. She wiped the back of her hand across her face and gave a big sniff.

"I know you have to go, I just *wish* you didn't."

He took her hands between his and kissed her tears away before he said, "I feel the same way. Come with me, Ursula. Be my wife, not as a ruse, but for real."

Her heart thumped hard, causing blood to roar in her ears. Jubilation and devastation warred in her mind.

"Tom, you know I can't. My family is here. Anna, Lotte, Mutter. They need me as much as I need them." She put her arms around his neck and looked into his eyes. "I have to stay, not only for them but for others who need my help. You have seen how terrible things are. If I turn my back now, without doing my share, that makes me a coward, worse than the Nazis themselves."

Tom shook his head. "You're not a coward, Ursula. You are by far the bravest, most determined, gentle, caring, upright, honest, and loyal person I've ever met."

Unwilling to give in to the temptation to just follow him and leave all her sorrows behind, she added, "I would be as unwelcome in your country as you are in mine. What would your superiors say if you brought home a German girl, Flying Officer Westlake?"

He hesitated and she could feel how torn he was between serving his country and wanting to be with her. "We could both stay in Sweden, we'd be safe there. Wait out the war..."

"Wouldn't that make you a coward?" Ursula looked up at Tom and gave him a gentle kiss.

He gave a deep sigh.

"I have to stay, and you need to go home," she said.

"I'll wait for you." The words burst from him. "I'll come and get you once we've won the war."

A tear spilled from her eye, then a second was followed by thousands more. "I'll wait for you, Tom. I love you."

They kissed one last time and then Tom turned to pass the border post. She waved after him as he passed without a problem and continued toward the ship with the Swedish flag.

When she could no longer see him, Ursula wandered aimlessly along the coastline looking at the water until she flopped down onto a patch of sand and cried until all the tears were gone. Then she got up and embarked on the long journey back home to her mother and Anna.

She sat on the train, enduring the long monotonous ride home. The world flashed past her through the windows, a blur of greens and browns. For the first time in weeks, Ursula had no sense of anxiety. During the multiple identification checks, she had not once stiffened in fear. Everything had worked out – Tom was safe, and so were she and her family.

It would be so easy to return to normalcy, to never step another toe out of line and pretend she did not know all the terrible things she did. But the war was no closer to ending, really, than when it had started. Ursula now understood her purpose and role within it: to help those who needed it in any way she could, regardless of the personal consequences.

She remembered the moment she'd first seen Tom hiding in the crack in the prison wall and hadn't called the alarm on him, as she should have done. In hindsight, that was the moment her life changed irrevocably. The turning point when she'd stopped being an obedient citizen who never asked questions, and had become a woman who aligned her actions with her moral compass, regardless of the consequences for her own life.

Despite public wisdom, there truly was no difference between Germans, English, even Jews. Everyone was hoping to survive this horrible war, and some did awful things that could only be justified in the light of the greater good. She had no illusions whatsoever that Tom would soon be back in the skies over her city, dropping his deadly cargo, perhaps even killing someone she knew. But who was she to judge him? What he did was done to serve his country, to protect the ones he loved. Just not her. She was the enemy.

They might love each other, but that didn't change one thing in the greater scheme of things.

Ursula got off the train in Berlin, determined to tell Pfarrer

Bernau that she wanted to continue to be a part of his network, helping wherever she was needed. A smile appeared on her lips as she walked the last block to her home. Determination and a newfound purpose in life energized her steps.

She arrived at the apartment and threw herself through the door, "Mutter, Anna, I'm home!"

Nobody answered. That was strange. Since the door hadn't been locked, they must be at home. Ursula entered the kitchen and found her mother and sister sitting in an embrace, crying.

"What has happened?" she asked, shock spreading across her face.

Mutter looked up, tears streaming down her face. "Lydia called," her mother said, her words blurred by sobs. "Lotte…" She couldn't go on as sobs wracked her.

No.

Lotte. Her baby sister. Pieces of her heart shattered and broke away as her mind considered each and every possibility.

"What? What's wrong?" Ursula pleaded, unable to stand the not knowing another second.

Finally, Anna looked up at her. "Lotte has disappeared."

WAR GIRL LOTTE is the story about Lotte's ordeals. She thinks there's nothing worse than boredom in the godforsaken village Kleindorf where her mother has sent her into banishment. But after a rescue mission for Jewish children gone wrong, she soon finds out there are plenty things worse…

Read War Girl Lotte now.

THE NEWEST BOOK in this series Stolen Childhood is currently only available as part of the collection "The Road to Liberation - Trials and Triumphs of WWII"

We wrote the six books in this collection to commemorate the 75th anniversary of Victory Day in Europe.

All events and celebrations have been cancelled due to the Corona pandemic, but we believe, remembering is now more important than ever and have therefore decided to keep the price for the entire 992-page book at 99ct until release day.

Please help us spread the word and send a glimmer of hope around the world:

Preorder the book here and let everyone know about it.

AUTHOR'S NOTES

Dear Reader,

Thank you so much for reading WAR GIRL URSULA.

While writing *Unwavering* (Book 3 in the Love and Resistance in WW2 Germany Trilogy), I read through the many letters my grandmother sent during her time in prison.

She mentioned twice a prison guard whom the prisoners called "Blonde Angel". She didn't say much, just something along the lines of, "The Blonde Angel allowed me an extra 15 minutes of visit time" or "The Blonde Angel said women aren't executed anymore". But those two sentences intrigued me enough to start wondering what kind of person the Blonde Angel might have been and why she became a prison guard, of all professions.

I have no idea about her real name, but I created Ursula Hermann as homage to the real life person who brought a modicum of comfort to the lives of my grandmother and the other inmates. Apart from the reference to her nickname, the person of Ursula Hermann is entirely fictional.

Pfarrer Bernau, the priest, whom you may remember from *Unwavering* as well, was modeled after the Catholic priest Buchholz and his Protestant colleague Poelchau, who both worked in Plötzensee and belonged to the resistance.

During an air raid on the night of September 3rd 1943, a large portion of the prison was destroyed. In the ensuing chaos four prisoners who'd been sentenced to death managed to escape. I took this real event as inspiration for Ursula and Tom's story. You can read more about the role of the Plötzensee prison in the Nazi terror here:

http://www.gedenkstaette-ploetzensee.de/07_e.html

ALSO BY MARION KUMMEROW

Love and Resistance in WW2 Germany

Unrelenting

Unyielding

Unwavering

Turning Point (Spin-off Love)

War Girl Series

Downed over Germany (Prequel)

War Girl Ursula (Book 1)

War Girl Lotte (Book 2)

War Girl Anna (Book 3)

Trouble Brewing (Book 4)

Reluctant Informer (Book 5)

Fatal Encounter (Book 6)

Uncommon Sacrifice (Book 7)

Bitter Tears (Book 8)

Secrets Revealed (Book 9)

Together at Last (Book 10)

Endless Ordeal (Book 11)

Berlin Fractured

From the Ashes (Book 1)

On the Brink (Book 2)

Historical Romance

Second Chance at First Love

Find all my books here:

http://www.kummerow.info

CONTACT ME

I truly appreciate you taking the time to read (and enjoy) my books. And I'd be thrilled to hear from you!
If you'd like to get in touch with me you can do so via

Twitter:
http://twitter.com/MarionKummerow

Facebook:
http://www.facebook.com/AutorinKummerow

Website
http://www.kummerow.info

Manufactured by Amazon.ca
Bolton, ON